THE HIDDEN GRAVE

A HARRIET HARPER THRILLER - BOOK 2

DOMINIKA BEST

THE HIDDEN GRAVE

Harriet Harper Thriller series - Book 2

This is a work of fiction. Any resemblance to actual persons living or dead, businesses, events or locales is purely coincidental.

ISBN: 978-1-949674-07-1

www.dominikabest.com

First Edition

For Dave
without you, none of this would be possible

ALSO BY DOMINIKA BEST

Harriet Harper Thriller Series

The Creek Killer

The Hidden Grave

The Broken Trail

The Night Blinder

Ghosts of Los Angeles

The Haunting of Sunshine House

The Haunting of Eva Murphy

The Haunting of Alexas Hotel

PROLOGUE

September 23, 1994

Lauren Harper sighed in happiness when the sign for the Tamolitch Trailhead appeared. The week before had been a busy one with classes, and she was thrilled to be getting out of town.

Tim Ledeyen pulled the Subaru into the graveled parking lot.

"Whoop! We got here in record time," she said.

Tim had invited her and Stephanie Rogers to come on a weekend camping trip, and Lauren had agreed to it before he even finished asking. Stephanie jumped in on it as well.

They decided to start hiking to the Tamolitch Pool in the Willamette National Forest first, then going onto Koosah and Sahalie Falls before finding a campsite for the night.

Lauren had been to another part of the Willamette National Forest the weekend before and swore she'd be back when she could. And here she was. Thanks to Tim.

She rolled down the window and breathed in deep. The scent of pine and wet, loamy earth hit her nostrils. This air was so different from the Los Angeles air she'd grown up in. The extra oxygen made her both dizzy and hyper.

"Thank you so much for inviting us, Tim," she said.

"I'm so glad that you said yes," he said.

Stephanie turned to Lauren from the front passenger seat and grinned. "The stress is almost gone," she sighed.

"Wait until we start walking," Tim said. He turned the car off.

Lauren had only been in Oregon for three weeks, and already she'd fallen in love with it. She'd been worried about feeling like she belonged in a place so different from where she'd grown up, but so far it had been surprisingly easy to make friends.

Lauren and Stephanie met in their Psychology 101 class two weeks ago and clicked immediately. Stephanie was from San Diego and loved surfing as much as Lauren did. They became fast friends over the fact that two beach bum girls from Southern California had become landlocked Oregonians when they chose Oregon State.

Tim was also in their Psychology 101 class and was in one of Stephanie's discussion groups. He was a native Oregonian. Having grown up about an hour outside of Eugene in a small town, Tim reminded Lauren of the consummate mountain man. His curly blonde hair reached his shoulders, and he sported a bushy beard. His uniform was a plaid button-down shirt, jeans, and hiking boots. She'd never seen him wear anything else.

They'd had lunch together several times over the last two weeks, and they all got along as if they'd known each other forever. He'd suggested the trip days ago and with all the drama Lauren had going with her dorm-mate, Jackie, she'd jumped at the chance.

Lauren focused back on the glory of the woods in front of her. Jackie's crazy would not impede her joy at being back here.

Lauren rolled her window closed and bounded out of her seat. She stretched her calves and made some small jumps. Feeling the burn of activity in her body, she stretched her arms high into the air and breathed in deep.

This day would be glorious.

They'd driven for close to two hours and apparently, everyone else was stiff, too. Tim and Stephanie did their own version of stretches as Lauren surveyed the small parking lot. It was more of a dirt patch really, with five other cars parked haphazardly around them.

Not as busy as she'd expected from reading about how popular the Tamolitch Pool was. It wasn't even ten o'clock yet though, and Lauren preferred fewer people anyway.

"Are you going to tell me what happened with Jackie?" Stephanie asked as Lauren leaned into the back seat and grabbed her backpack.

"I don't know if I want to get into that right now," Lauren said.

"Jackie is your roommate, right?" Tim asked.

"Yes," Lauren said and slung her backpack on her shoulders. Her friends were waiting expectantly for her reply. Lauren shrugged, answering. "She's really upset with me that I walked in on her and her boyfriend having sex a couple of nights ago. She wasn't even supposed to be home. It was an honest mistake."

"Doesn't seem like something anyone should be so upset about," Tim remarked.

"I might've been a little tipsy and left the door open longer than I should have. I was shocked to see them, honestly. I guess her boyfriend really bit into her about it. Per usual girl crap, she's taking it out on me," Lauren said.

Anger flashed at the memory of Jackie yelling at her the day before. Lauren had struggled not to roll her eyes at her shrieking dormmate. She had found the whole episode ridiculous and overdramatic. When she told Jackie that and mentioned her boyfriend was uptight, Jackie hadn't taken it well.

"That's lame. And it's even worse that you have to live in a tiny eight by eight room with her," Stephanie said.

"I'm so glad I'm gone this weekend. I'm hoping she'll have some space to cool down," Lauren said as Tim locked the car.

He led them towards the entrance to the trailhead.

They'd walked for close to five minutes when Lauren and Stephanie found Tim's pace much faster than their own. He kept walking ahead a decent distance and then having to stop.

"You can go on ahead. We'll catch up," Lauren called after him.

He waved as his body lost much of its tension. He sped up and the distance grew between him and the girls.

"I hope he's not planning to race the entire time," Stephanie said.

Lauren shrugged. "It's his hike too, I guess."

"I don't want to pick up the pace," Stephanie said.

"Neither do I," Lauren said.

"Perfect. I hoped you'd say that."

Lauren smiled and tilted her face to the sun dappling

through the tall Douglas Firs. The pine needles crunched under their feet. The birds chirped in the distance. Small animals scuttled about in the undergrowth searching for their breakfasts.

Lauren put her hand on her stomach as it rumbled at the thought of breakfast. She should have eaten more than a handful of almonds this morning.

She pulled her backpack around to her front and stuck her hand in to find her water bottle. She rummaged around and frowned.

"Oh crap. I left my water bottle in the backseat," she said.

"That's not going to work," Stephanie said.

"No, it's not." Lauren stopped walking. "Hey, Tim!" she called out.

Tim stopped his forward march and turned back around. The look on his face told Lauren he hadn't realized how far ahead he'd gotten.

"I forgot my water bottle in the car."

Tim briskly walked back to them and his face showed annoyance. But Lauren wasn't walking miles without water.

"We've only been walking about ten minutes. I can run back and get it in half the time, I swear."

"You're going to run?" Tim asked, somewhat dubiously.

"I'll sprint." Lauren flashed him her best smile.

He finally smiled back. "I'm going to hold you to that," Tim said.

Lauren took off her backpack and threw it at his feet. "I'll run faster without it. Be back in a flash," she said.

Tim pulled the keys out of his pocket and handed them to her.

"You aren't going to leave us stranded here, right?" Stephanie asked.

"I would never," Lauren said and winked.

She whipped around and sprinted away from her friends. Her legs pumped beneath her as she flew down the path, enjoying the stretching of her muscles and the wind in her face. She kept up that pace the entire way back and found herself in the parking lot way faster than she'd expected.

Only two vehicles remained in the lot. Tim's Subaru and a white-paneled van parked several spaces away.

Who in the world would drive a paneled van to a hiking trail?

Unease slithered around her stomach. Unfortunately, the van was on the side of Tim's car she needed to get to.

You're being ridiculous, she thought. There's no one here.

The van standing empty bolstered her own argument.

She wished there were other cars in the lot. They'd only been gone fifteen minutes and Lauren found it odd the cars she'd seen in the parking lot when they arrived had already driven off. There had to be another trail nearby that used the parking lot as well.

She stepped forward and decided to use the driver's side to look for her water. She wouldn't go near the van.

She raised her hand to click the door open when she heard footsteps behind her coming from the trail she'd just left.

Goosebumps spread up her arms as she froze.

"I need your help," a child's voice said from behind her.

Lauren frowned. Her unease grew and a lump formed in her throat.

A child lost in the woods. Was that even possible?

She glanced over at the van. It stood silent.

Everything in her suddenly burned with the desire to run. Get the hell out of here. It's a trap. Something's wrong.

Instead, she turned around.

"Are you lost?"

1

DAY 1 - THURSDAY, SEPTEMBER 27, 2018

Detective Harriet Harper leaned back in the passenger seat of the rental car and closed her eyes. The strong sense of deja vu made her head spin. She was back again and hoped this time, the results would be different. Her sister, Lauren Harper, was still missing. Harri had come to Oregon every year to find Lauren's remains and she'd failed every time.

Harri and Jake Tepesky had picked up the rental car from the Portland Airport and were headed to their first destination. She'd programmed an address into her phone.

At least on this trip, Jake Tepesky, her sister's best friend in high school, was with Harri. He had been an FBI profiler for the last fifteen years, and she hoped his expertise might finally shake the truth loose. A tall order, she knew, because Lauren had been missing since 1994.

Harri was no slouch with cold cases. Her work with the Cold Case Unit in the Los Angeles Police Department regularly had her searching for killers who'd gotten away with murder years before.

This time would be different, she thought hopefully.

"You ready?" Jake asked.

Harri checked the back seat to make sure she'd grabbed all her luggage. "I'm all set. Thanks again for driving."

"I'm glad I can help. I know it's been quite the few weeks for you."

"Sorry we didn't get to meet over Lauren's case notes," she said.

Harri hadn't seen Jake Tepesky much in the last two weeks. The Creek Killer case she'd been on had overwhelmed her with its endless intra-agency meetings between the FBI, LAPD, and the Imperial Valley Sheriff's Department. She and Jake had become reacquainted through another FBI profiler on the Creek Killer case and had reconnected over Lauren's disappearance.

She'd done her best to keep pace of all the new developments on one of the biggest serial killer cases in Los Angeles in recent years, but the various agencies would be out there for months cataloging the evidence left behind and exhuming the numerous victims.

The count stood at ten last she'd heard. At least a number of missing person cases would be closed. The killer had left behind driver's licenses of some of his victims, which prompted the renewed search on the property.

Harri wished she could get that kind of closure for her sister, Lauren. She had disappeared without a trace on a hike to the Tamolitch Falls over twenty-five years ago. This weekend was the anniversary of her disappearance.

She pressed her hand as sudden pain flared in her chest. She never felt well coming up here. Harri stared out the window at the beautiful scenery of the changing colors of the fall season, a cacophony of oranges, yellows, and reds.

"I went through the case files three times." Jake interrupted her thoughts.

"And?" she asked.

"You're a very thorough investigator," Jake said.

Harri gave him a small smile. For all her investigating skills, she had exhausted every single lead and had come up with nada. Nothing.

"Did you find anything that I missed?" she asked.

"There wasn't much. Lauren had been at school for only three weeks and no one knew her very well. She hadn't had time to make any close friends. You thoroughly researched her roommate, Jacqueline Strauss, and the boyfriend, Charlie Burke. You tracked down the alibis. They were solid."

"I exhausted those leads. Charlie Burke played soccer the afternoon Lauren went missing. About twenty-five players swore he was on the field. Jackie pledged her sorority and thirty girls accounted for her movement."

"I don't think it was anyone she knew."

"You're thinking stranger abduction?"

"More like crime of opportunity."

"I came to a similar realization. That's why it's been so hard to track down," Harri said.

"They tend to be. The kidnappers always slip up somewhere, though. We have to find where."

"Do you think I'm wrong about the burial site?" Harri asked. She'd asked a non-profit group of scientists trained to search for hidden graves to join them this time. It had taken Harri years to set up since she didn't have specific proof that her sister was buried in the same place as she disappeared.

"Where do we go first?" Jake asked.

"I always start with Tim Ledeyen. We've become friends over the years. He lets me know about similar cases that crop up in the city. And there's always the hope he'll remember something else from that day."

"How does he feel about being your first stop?" Jake asked.

Harri flushed.

The last few years she'd come up, Tim had been less than happy to see her. He'd barely known Lauren, but he'd joined Harri's search for her sister the first five years she'd come up. Recently, Harri had felt a certain coldness from Tim when they'd met. She believed Tim wanted to get on with his life. He'd moved on.

She could never do that. She needed to bring her sister's body home. Harri had no doubt that Lauren died all those years ago. It was a matter of finding her remains now and trying to piece together what happened back then.

"We're driving to Tim Ledeyen's now or to the bed and breakfast?" Jake asked.

"Tim's, unless you wanted to stop somewhere for a pee or coffee, or something."

"No, I'm good," Jake said and grinned. His handsome face lit up with a smile.

The morning sun created a halo around his face, and Harri's stomach suddenly did a couple of unwanted flip flops. Jake had been her sister's best friend in high school. They were here to find Lauren. There was no time for this nonsense, she thought. They'd enjoyed an intimate dinner together some weeks back, and Harri thought some spark was ignited for a second. Looking back at it now she was convinced it was in her imagination.

Harri hadn't slept in weeks and this trip always did

strange things to her moods and her levelheadedness. Oregon was a fever dream every time she came up here.

"I booked us rooms at the Daniels Inn off the McKenzie Highway, Route 126. Tim Ledeyen's house is a few miles outside of Eugene. He's on our way to the Inn."

"Great, and the scientists? Where are we meeting them?"

"The pig team is also staying at the Daniels Inn."

"I thought they were called NecroFind?" Jake asked. "Although the pig team is more descriptive. Why are they called that?"

"They use pigs in their research. Bury them for long periods of time to see the changes to the surrounding site. I guess the nickname stuck."

"How big is the team?" Jake asked.

"I have a botanist, a geologist, and a dog handler with a bloodhound coming. Along with the head scientist, of course."

"Bloodhound?"

"Her name is Amy. Supposedly, she's been able to find graves this old before in Colorado," she said.

"Can't wait to meet them all," Jake said. "If you want to take a nap or something, I'll totally understand. I know you haven't gotten much sleep over the last few weeks."

"It's been crazy. That last case is far from over," she said.

"You mentioned you were coordinating between the various jurisdictions?" he asked.

Harri knew Jake wouldn't ask too many questions on an ongoing case. He'd been FBI. At the same time, the discovery of the new bodies by the field team had been all over the newspapers.

"As much as I could. I had to hand it over to another person on the team as I was coming up here. I tried to get everything done, but the case was moving too fast for me. They'll be there for months, just cataloging. To be honest, I was relieved to be coming up here." That wasn't entirely true. At least, she'd be able to get some sleep here.

"Rest then. We should be there in an hour."

"I'll try to do that, Jake. Thank you," she said.

"Do you mind if I put on some music?"

"Better not be Green Day," she said.

That made Jake guffaw. "Haven't listened to them in years. I'll put in something classical. I think that'll suit both of us."

Harri looked at him and saw his jaw clenched. This was hard for him, too. He had come up that first year to search and never joined in again. He never came back. Lauren had been his best friend through most of high school. She knew they'd been close and talked to each other almost every day that first month of college.

"Thank you again for coming with me. This can't be easy for you, either."

"I want to find her too," he said

He turned on the music. Something soft and romantic. The motion of the car made Harri's eyes droop, she let herself be dragged down into the darkness.

"Harri, we're here," Jake said.

Harri opened her eyes and squinted at the harsh late morning light. He'd pulled into the driveway of a small Cape Cod home nestled between tall fir trees. Tim Ledeyen owned four acres behind his house.

"What else do I need to know about Tim Ledeyen?" he asked.

"He's an Oregon native who grew up outside of Eugene. He finished the University of Oregon and became an accountant. He has a wife named Molly, and a teenage son named Dan, a teenager. He's never been in trouble, not even a speeding ticket."

"That doesn't mean much," he said.

"True," Harri admitted.

"What kind of questions you typically ask him?"

"I take him through the timeline each time. He's remembered little things over the years."

"Like?"

"Cars he remembers passing him on the way to the park as he drove into the parking lot. Bits of a license plate. Bits and pieces like that. They haven't amounted to much honestly."

"Are you going to introduce me as an FBI agent?"

"No, if that's okay. I want to keep it personal. You were Lauren's best friend from high school. That's all he needs to know."

"All right then. I'll take your lead," he said.

They left the sanctuary of the car and walked up the paved path to the front door. Harri raised her hand to knock on the door but it opened before she made contact. Molly's tear-stained face peered out from a darkened hallway.

"Molly, what's wrong?" Harri asked.

"Dan never came home last night. It hasn't been twenty-four hours and the police won't let us report him missing, but he would never do this to me. I know there's something wrong."

Jake and Harri glanced at each other.

"May we come in?" Harri asked.

Molly stepped aside and Harri and Jake entered. Molly motioned them to the left, towards the kitchen.

"Is Tim home?" Harri asked.

Molly shook her head no.

"Is he out looking for Dan?"

"Yes. He's been out since six this morning. He knew that you were coming today because, obviously, you come every year. He's sorry to have missed you, but we are just out of our minds with worry."

Harri put her hand on Molly's arm.

"Maybe I can help. I have a contact at the Eugene Police Department. He might be able to expedite the process somewhat. Get your statement."

"Yes. God, please. We need more people searching. He's only sixteen."

"Are you sure that he's not with friends?" Jake asked.

Molly shook her head vigorously. "He's had some problems with drugs in the last few months. We sent him to rehab and he was doing really well. He was keeping with his curfew of ten o'clock every night. He wasn't hanging out with any of his old friends." Molly paused and took a breath. "Dan called us last night to tell us that he was coming straight home."

"Where was he coming from?" Harri asked.

Jake sat silently next to her.

"He'd been at a job interview in Eugene. He was hoping to become a barista at one of the local coffee shops near the University. It was a big step for him, and we were very excited, and he told us he was coming straight home and then he disappeared," she said in a rush.

Harri heard the hysteria rising in her voice. "Did you call the coffee shop to see if he made it there?" Harri asked, taking a small notebook out of her pocket.

"Of course. The woman manager answered. He'd interviewed with her. She said he did great and was their top candidate."

"What time did he leave?"

"She said around five-thirty yesterday evening," Molly said, finally getting herself somewhat under control.

"How did he leave?" Harri asked, jotting the time down.

"I don't know," Molly shook her head. "We don't know. His car was still in the parking lot. The manager told us after she went to look. That's when Tim tore out of here like a bat out of hell to see for himself."

Harri nodded and bit her lip. His car still being there wasn't a good sign. But he could have run into one of his old friends from the drug days and fell off the wagon. A few months sober was not that long of a time. Harri assumed that's what the Eugene police would say. But Molly did not need to hear that right now.

"And Tim is still in Eugene right now looking for him?" she asked.

Molly nodded. Her tears started again. "Please help us. He's only sixteen and has had such a difficult time," Molly pleaded, tears running down her face.

Harri looked at Jake and took her phone out of her pocket. "Let me see what I can do."

Molly burst into tears again and Jake sat there patting her on the hand. He had a calming effect on Molly, who leaned back in her chair and breathed.

"We will help any way we can," Jake said.

2

DAY 1

Richard Miller stood in his kitchen gazing out into the backyard where his son, little Richie, was playing with the family dog. He had made a life for himself despite all the odds. Claire, his wife, came into the kitchen and smiled at him. He had been lucky to meet a woman like her. He hadn't told her everything that had happened to him, but she knew enough, and she understood why he screamed out during the night.

"Everything okay, Richard?" she asked and ran her hand along his shoulder.

"Thinking of what I want to do with my day today. I'm thinking of fixing up that patch of garden in the back. Maybe put in some greens. We could all use some healthy vegetables in our lives," he said and grinned.

She shook her head at him. "Your day off? Why don't you relax and go read a book," she said.

Her head disappeared into the fridge as he turned to look back at his son. If she only knew that he could never relax. The pain of what had happened to him came rolling into him the moment he stopped doing. His only way of escaping his past was to keep the forward momentum going. To constantly be on the move and doing stuff, didn't matter what kind of stuff.

"I'm gonna go work on the garden," he said.

Claire peeked over the refrigerator door. "Will you call Richie inside? I think it's getting a little bit too cold out there for him."

"Absolutely," he said and went over to the kitchen table where his jacket was hanging. "Looks like it might rain," he said.

The gray sky looked more ominous than normal. Oregon was known for its rain fall and Eugene had its fair share of gray skies and incessant rain. It didn't bother him much, but when the sun was out, his mood got even darker.

The phone rang. Richard flinched at the sound.

"You sure you're doing all right?" Claire asked him.

"I get jumpy sometimes," he said, trying not to get too defensive. He reached over to his cell phone and looked down at the screen. He didn't recognize the number.

He was waiting for a phone call from the bank, though, and maybe this was it. He clicked on the button and put the phone to his ear.

"Hello?" he asked.

At first, he heard only a distant static. Then a voice, hollow, insistent, whispered. "It's starting again. Be ready. It's starting again."

The caller on the other end clicked off.

Richard stood with the phone still to his ear, his heart pounding.

It couldn't be.

Over the years, he'd heard through the grapevine that

the group had scattered. That some had been caught, and the others had gone underground.

It was starting again.

He broke into a cold sweat. His heart pounded in his chest and he inadvertently pressed his hand down, trying to calm himself the only way he knew how.

It was starting again.

He looked over at his son.

"We shouldn't let him play outside by himself like that," he said. "There's too many dangerous people around."

He went over to the patio door and opened it.

"Richie, come back inside," he said.

The boy's face screwed up with concern when he heard the tone of his father's voice.

"I'm coming, Dad," he said.

"Right now."

The boy ran towards him, the dog on his heels.

It was starting again.

3

DAY 1 - EVENING

Detective Harri Harper pulled into an empty spot in the picturesque parking lot of Daniels Inn. It had been a much longer day than they expected.

After helping the Ledeyens file their missing child report, Harri introduced Tim and Molly to Detective Gavin French, her longtime friend in the Eugene Police Department. He hadn't been convinced their son had met with foul play, but he worried the boy overdosed somewhere and needed help. Harri and Jake finally left the Ledeyens to get ready for their morning meeting with NecroFind the next day.

"You weren't joking about the decor," Jake said, interrupting her thoughts.

The inn resembled a hunting lodge with a pair of antlers of long-dead deer hanging on both sides of the front door.

Jake whistled beside her. Harri had been coming here for so many years she'd become immune to its odd rustic charm.

"It's really nice inside. The owner, Mack Collins, is really hospitable in that old-timey middle-of-nowhere way. It's the nicest place near the Tamolitch Falls entrance."

Jake cocked his head, deep in thought. "This is the place we all stayed at when we searched for her that fall, isn't it?"

She wondered if he'd remember it.

"Yes, it is. It was called the Tammy Lodge back then."

"You stay here every year?"

"Yes. Mack knows me well." Harri managed a small smile. Her stomach churned as it always did on the first day of her pilgrimage. Would this time be any different?

"The dining room closes in about twenty minutes," Harri said, checking the time. "If we hurry, we can eat a hot meal."

Jake was out of the car in a flash, Harri hurrying after him.

"Hungry?"

"Starving," he called back to her.

Harri clicked the car doors closed behind her and followed him inside.

"This is the best steak I've ever eaten," Jake said as he inhaled the rib-eye on the plate in front of him.

"I'm surprised you can taste it with how fast you're eating," Harri observed.

"You're right. I should slow down," Jake said, but didn't slow down at all.

Harri picked at the grilled chicken she'd gotten with her salad. Her stomach was too unsettled and even though she was hungry, none of the food was appetizing to her.

Besides their table, the dining room was empty. The staff had made an exception for them thanks to Mack pleading their case as the kitchen was closing right as they rushed inside.

She gulped down her second glass of water.

"You aren't eating," Jake observed.

"My stomach isn't up to it."

"I get that."

"I always think it's going to be easier, but it never is."

"I wouldn't expect it to get any easier. When we do find her, your feelings will evolve, but they'll always be there."

"I know it's not healthy to push things down. Sometimes, it's just unbearable, though." Harri surprised herself for revealing this much to him.

"I understand the pain of losing my friend. I can't imagine what it would be like for it to be my sister. I know the pain flares up. Sometimes, it just seems to come out of nowhere. For me, it's like a hole that can't be filled."

It was the closest anyone had ever gotten to describing what the loss of Lauren felt like for her. They sat in silence for a moment.

Jake pointed at her chicken. "Eat. You need your energy for tomorrow. Brain doesn't work on no nutrients."

Harri cut off a small piece of chicken and put it in her mouth. She chewed methodically, focusing hard on not gagging on the chewy piece of meat. Jake was right. She needed all her faculties firing for the upcoming week.

"Tell me about tomorrow," Jake said as he dug into his scalloped potatoes. The rich smell of the dish wafted towards her and made her nauseous.

"We're meeting with Dr. Susan Liewicke and her

team in the parking lot at eight in the morning. She's the head of this group. I'm not sure which scientists will be there tomorrow, but I know Amy the bloodhound will be."

"I did a little research on these folks. Their success rate is impressive, especially considering how incredibly hard it is to find old graves."

Harri breathed in deep. "I want to hope that this time we will find her." Her voice came out small. Vulnerability washed over her, and she fought back the tears.

Jake put down his fork and grasped her hand in his. The warmth of his touch soothed her. Harri gave him a half-smile as his eyes held hers.

"I'm so happy we met again," he said. "That I'm here." His voice was gruffer than it had been a moment ago.

"I am too, Jake." Tears rolled down her cheek. The warmth of his touch radiated through her body and her breath caught. His gaze intensified and Harri pulled her hand away, wiping her tears. This wasn't the time. Not here. Not now.

"You knew her probably better than I did," Harri said.

Jake nodded and looked down at his food.

The moment was gone.

She'd rejected him and she could see his hurt. Her heart thumped. She was so happy to have him here, by her side.

"Thank you for coming with me," Harri said.

"I'm sorry I didn't come sooner," Jake said.

"You were smart. You moved on."

"I didn't move on," he shook his head. "I pushed it all down and pushed away. You know what the therapists say about that."

"I might have an idea," Harri said. She cracked a smile.

The mood shifted.

The comfort between the two was back again.

"I've seen videos of how they do the search. I'm expecting we'll be there all day. Mack said he'd pack up sandwiches and snacks," Harri said.

"How much of the area are we going to search?" he asked and threw his napkin over his plate.

"I've mapped out an area between the place Tim's keys were found and the spot where Tim and Stephanie waited for her. My assumption is that she never left those woods."

Harri chewed on her lip.

"What's wrong?"

"What if my assumption is wrong?"

"Your case file is as complete as any I've ever read. I know you've gone through it with laser focus. You've followed every strand."

Harri smiled. "Thank you for saying that. I appreciate that more than you know."

"I mean it. Really."

Harri surprised herself with a yawn. "We should get to bed. From what I've seen of this team we're going to be out there until we find something."

Jake nodded and stood up. "Good plan."

Harri followed suit with a groan. Her body ached and bad.

I will do my best, Lauren. I promise, she thought.

4

DAY 2 - FRIDAY, SEPTEMBER 28, 2018

Detective Harri Harper and Jake Tepesky pulled into the busy parking lot of the Tamolitch Falls trailhead. They had awoken to a slight rain and Harri worried that the search might be put off for another day. But when she called Dr. Susan Liewicke, the team leader of NecroFind, she was assured they could go ahead with no issues. The rain had finally subsided somewhat on their arrival even though everything dripped.

"They don't look like the rain has affected them at all," Jake said gesturing to the small crowd.

There were about ten people under the makeshift tent of the staging area, their attention focused on maps on the table. Harri noticed Detective Gavin French and a deputy talking to a tall gray-haired woman.

"I have to assume that's Dr. Susan Liewicke," Harri said.

"Cute dog," Jake said.

Harri hadn't noticed the bloodhound at first, but then she came sniffing around the outer edge of the tented area. She was exactly what Harri expected a bloodhound cadaver dog to look like. Long ears and droopy jowls. Amy the dog was surprisingly big, close to a hundred pounds. Harri and Jake stepped out of the car and joined the rest of the search team.

"I thought we would be here early," Harri started.

"We wanted to set up early because we have so much to cover," the statuesque woman said.

Harri nodded, admiring the silver sheen of her hair. This woman had no issues with growing old. She wore her age with pride.

"I am Dr. Susan Liewicke, the team leader on this search," she said.

Harri shook her outstretched hand. "Detective Harriet Harper and this is Jake Tepesky. He's a former profiler from the Behavioral Science Unit at Quantico. He's a friend lending his expertise and not here in a professional capacity."

"Hi everyone," Jake said.

"Thank you so much for coming out here with your team, Dr. Liewicke. I know the parameters don't exactly match your typical searches," Harri said.

"Call me Dr. Susan. Everyone does." She flashed Harri a smile. "And we're always up for a challenge," Dr. Susan said. "Let me introduce you to the rest of the team."

"This is Dr. Jasmine Brand. She's a geologist with expertise on the Oregon terrain having grown up here. She's an expert in this entire region. She's with the University of Oregon," Dr. Susan said, gesturing to a dark-haired, olive-skinned woman.

Harri wondered if Dr. Brand was from one of the Native American tribes in the area. "Are you a local?" Harri asked.

"I am. I'm from the Burns area. Specifically, the Burns Paiute Tribe," Dr. Brand said.

"Thanks for sharing your expertise with us," Harri said. She took note to get contact information from Dr. Brand. If this search today was a bust, the woman would be a goldmine of information about these woods.

"I'm really happy to be here," she said.

Dr. Susan beamed and turned to an older gentleman to her left. "Then we have Dr. Robert Gustafson, our botanist." Dr. Susan said.

Dr. Gustafson appeared to be in his 50s and sported a grizzly gray-white beard and dark hair pulled back in a ponytail. To Harri, he looked like he spent a lot of time in the woods. His vest and pants sprouted pockets from every imaginable surface. All he was missing was a walking stick.

He held out his hand.

"Very nice to meet you, Dr. Gustafson," Harri said.

"Oh, I'm just Robbie, Detective," he said.

Harri nodded and turned to the dog handler and the bloodhound. The dog handler was a man in his 30s with curly sandy brown hair and laughing brown eyes. He was a big man and reminded her of a firefighter or maybe a soldier.

"This is Doug Kessler and his cadaver dog, Amy. He's an expert tracker as is Amy, of course." Dr. Susan continued.

"Thanks for the kind words Doc, but it's all Amy here. I follow her lead and understand her language." He rubbed the dog's head affectionately.

"Doug has been on the most searches out of this team," Dr. Susan said.

"Outside of you, Dr. Susan. We're old-timers at this."

"Is the rain going to affect Amy's smell sense?" Harri asked.

"Heavy downpour keeps the scents down, but with this kind of light misting and drizzle we should be okay," Doug explained.

"I'm glad to hear that. I know this is such a long shot, I'm betting on any odds I can get," Harri said.

Susan motioned to the five younger people still surrounding the map table.

"These graduate students offered to come and help on the search. Jade, Cory, Matt, Gary, and Ava." Dr. Susan pointed to each one of them as she called out their names.

"Thank you all so much for coming out and helping," Harri said.

Most of them nodded, but no one said anything.

"Detective Harper," Detective Gavin French said from behind her.

Harri turned and shook Gavin's hand. "I wasn't sure if you were going to come on your own today," she said.

"I wanted to meet the NecroFind team. You guys have done incredible work around the country," he said to the cluster of scientists behind her.

"You've all already met?" Harri asked.

"Yup. We all got here early. Surprised you slept in."

Harri noted the teasing tone in his voice. "I'm here an hour early. Wasn't expecting all of you to beat me here," Harri said.

"We've given him a rundown on how we plan to execute the search today," Dr. Susan said.

"Yeah, they've given me some especially useful information on how to properly do grid searches. It's been a very worthwhile morning for me," Gavin said.

Gavin French was as dedicated a detective as they came and Harri knew he was sincere.

"And this here is Deputy Larry Delray. He's going to be making sure there are no passersby or lookie-loos. We've already posted signage closing off this parking lot to any traffic, but there's always a surprise or two. People get curious."

"I see you've gridded out the surrounding area. How are you starting?" Jake asked Dr. Susan.

Harri spied two Starbucks containers. "Coffee? Can I have some?" she asked Robbie the botanist.

"Help yourself," he said as Dr. Susan turned back to the maps on the table.

Harri poured herself and Jake each a cup. She handed him the black coffee as they drew closer to where Dr. Susan was pointing.

"We are starting in the area that Lauren Harper's keys were found by one of the witnesses. From that spot, we have drawn a grid in two-foot increments in every direction. We start at the keys and fan out."

"Is everybody ready?" Dr. Susan asked her team.

They all nodded.

"I'll take the first shift, then Robbie, and then Dr. Brand." Dr. Susan nodded to the grad students who prepared the wooden stakes, red ribbon, and twine.

They walked over to the mouth of the trailhead where the forest opened to the parking lot. Tim Ledeyen had found his keys right where the parking lot and forest met all those years ago. Dr. Susan dropped to her knees and bent down, her nose inches away from the spot.

The search began.

When each scientist finished their search, made notes, and moved on to the next square, one of the graduate students staked out the already searched terrain with the wooden stakes and twine. It was painstakingly slow work.

"I'm glad we're here all week," Harri whispered to Jake.

He nodded.

Doug Kessler and Amy were off to the side, doing their own preparations.

"You aren't working within the grid, are you?" Harri asked.

"No, I'm going to the end of the parking lot." He pointed to the left of the main trail, about thirty feet out. "Amy and I are going to start in the woods there and see what we find. I have a way to cover ground systematically, as well. I'm hoping we can pinpoint an area for all the docs to comb over. We'll work our way towards the keys without getting in the way of the docs."

"Good luck. I hope you find something," Harri said.

Doug patted Amy on the head. "If she's out there, Amy will find her. I absolutely believe in this beautiful girl." With that, he and Amy walked away from Harri and Jake, past the scientists and the trailhead, and followed the forest line. Once they reached the end of the parking lot, they stepped into the forest, Amy's nose low to the ground, and disappeared.

"What should we do?" Jake asked.

"Not get in their way and bring them coffee?" Harri quipped.

"Sounds like something we can handle."

Harri took a sip of the warm liquid, savoring the heat as she swallowed. The rain had stopped, but the air held a chill. Harri involuntarily shivered.

The sky hung low and dark above them. Drops of rain fell periodically from the branches and leaves nearby.

The place was silent and cold. Not like the day that Lauren disappeared. Tim recounted how excited he, Lauren, and Stephanie had been to get out there. How warm and sunny it had been. This weather was made for staying home.

Harri smelled the loamy dirt and her stomach flip-flopped. She hadn't eaten breakfast, her nerves turning her stomach sour. She closed her eyes and ran down her mental list of all the people she would re-interview, hopefully with something to go on. Some new piece of information she could throw out there to see who came out of the woodwork.

She opened her eyes to see Gavin standing next to her.

"Any news on Dan Ledeyen?" she asked.

"The missing addict?" Gavin asked.

"Yes," she said.

"Haven't located him yet," he said. "It's only a matter of time. I've seen cases like this before. I have a couple of uniforms going through the known flophouses in the area looking for him."

"Did anyone see him leaving the coffee shop?" Jake asked. "Nice to see you again, Detective French."

"You, too. Coffee any good?" he asked, pointing at Jake's cup.

"It's hot."

"Good enough for me." Gavin went over and poured himself a cup. "We did get a tip that he was seen getting into an early model pale-blue Prius. The woman didn't get a license plate number, of course. Once I'm done here, I'll see if any of our known heroin dealers sport that kind of ride."

"If he used, it's not good. He's been clean for

months," Harri said remembering Molly Ledeyen's sobbing face.

"That's how they overdose," Gavin said.

"Is it still a problem up here?" Jake asked.

"Worse than ever. Those poor parents. I'm holding out hope he's zonked out somewhere and lost track of the days."

"I'm with you on that hope," Harri said and watched as the scientists crawled deeper into the woods.

The morning went by with no significant finds. The team had found garbage, another set of keys, and a glove, but otherwise nothing they could use. Doug and Amy came up empty, but the team was still in good spirits.

The day had turned warmer and it was more pleasant to be outside. Harri and Jake had brought sandwiches from Daniels Inn for everybody. The sandwiches were good enough and the team tired enough, that most of lunch was spent in silence.

"Is the afternoon going to look similar to this morning?" Harri asked.

"That's right," Dr. Susan explained. "I know it looks like tedious work. We are gathering info on the type of soil that each quadrant has, how deep a hole could be dug out, any impressions of long-ago holes that have sunk, and created indents. Also, types of bug and growth activity that is typical around graves this old."

"And Doug, you and Amy are going to do the right side of the trail now?" Harri asked.

"That's right," Doug said.

As if Amy heard her name, she sat up and sniffed the air. She gave a small whine and pulled on the leash in

Doug's hand with her body towards the right. She whined again.

Doug watched Amy intently. "Are you sure, girl?" he asked her.

The dog chuffed and gave a little whine again.

"Amy's telling me she's smelling death. That's her sound for a cadaver." His brow furrowed. "She didn't notice it when we first got here, but the wind picked up from the right. It might be any dead thing, though."

He put down his partially eaten sandwich and loosened his hold on the dog. "I'm following, Amy."

Amy took off towards the right, sniffing furiously at the ground. She stopped at a spot around fifteen feet from the trailhead and then plunged into the forest again.

Harri held her breath.

Jake spoke up first. "Has it happened like this before with Amy?"

Dr. Susan frowned. "Not like this, no."

Could it be this easy? Was Amy, at this very moment, sniffing out a trail to a grave close to twenty-five years old? Harri could hardly believe it. Her heart thumped wildly in her chest and a bead of sweat rolled down her back. She didn't want to hope like this.

A whistle sounded off in the distance.

"Can you hear that?" Dr. Susan said.

"That's his whistle for a body," Robbie the botanist said.

All thoughts of lunch were long gone. Excitement rippled through the group.

Dr. Susan stood up from her seat, motioning to the graduate students to grab the wooden stakes.

"If we find remains, this is a crime scene. We must preserve all evidence so we can't go running in like a herd of elephants. Jade and I will create a route that's marked by stakes and twine that everyone can follow. We can limit the damage to the crime scene in that way. Detective French and Detective Harper will be coming along with us?" Dr. Susan asked.

Harri and Gavin nodded.

Jake held back, watching the entire team, his face shuttered and unreadable. He nodded at her. He was asking her if she was okay. Concern flickered in his eyes.

She nodded to him. This was what they both wanted. To bring Lauren home.

"We're right behind you, Dr. Susan," Harri said.

Dr. Susan and Jade walked to the spot Doug and Amy used to enter the forest. Jade hammered a wooden stake into the ground and tied the end of a thick, round roll of twine to it. Harri and Gavin watched as she made sure the knot was tight.

"I'm ready. After you, Dr. Susan," Jade said.

They entered the forest one by one.

They followed Dr. Susan as she carefully went step-by-step along a barely visible animal path. It didn't look like it was well-traveled, but there was enough of a path to walk on without too much underbrush.

Doug's whistle sounded every five seconds to help them navigate towards his location. After about five minutes of walking and fifteen stakes hammered into the ground, they found Doug and Amy standing off to the side of a large conifer tree.

"Oh no," Harri muttered. "Are you seeing what I'm seeing?" she asked no one in particular.

Gavin was right beside her. "That's a fresh body," he said.

They walked to within twenty feet from Doug and Amy.

Jade pounded the last wooden stake into the ground and tied the twine to it. She cut the roll loose and stared at the corpse.

Gavin pushed past her and made his way to Doug and Amy.

Harri couldn't hear what they were saying from this distance, but she was certain of what would be happening next. From her vantage point, she could see that the victim was a boy, aged thirteen or fourteen. He was dressed as if going to church, with neatly pressed khakis and a crisp white shirt.

Harri's heart pounded against her ribcage. The white shirt had barely any dirt on it. His face was clean, and his hair brushed. He looked to be sleeping more than dead. The killer had made a pillow for him out of the needles on the forest floor.

This was only the beginning was her first thought.

Harri's breath caught in her throat. The search for her sister would be coming to an abrupt halt. There was no way they could search alongside an active crime scene.

Gavin withdrew his cell phone from his pocket and checked for a signal. He dialed and put the phone to his ear. This place would be crawling with police and crime scene investigators within an hour.

Another killer preying on innocent victims. Another year where her sister would not be found.

Dr. Susan looked over to her, all excitement gone. Her face was pale and her eyes wide. Harri knew she'd never seen a murdered child before.

"I'm sorry," was all Harri could say.

5

DAY 2

The sun dipped below the trees as Harri was finally called to the area where Eugene Police Detective Lewis Robinson was taking statements from everyone at the scene. It had been an exceptionally long day of waiting. After they had left the body, Harri and Doug, Susan and Gavin all made their way out to the staging area.

Gavin had called the US Forest Service official that oversaw this specific part of the Willamette National Forest and the Eugene Police Department. He'd recognized the boy as Atticus Menlo, age thirteen, a boy who had gone missing in Eugene last week. One of Gavin's friends, Detective Louis Robinson had been on the case and he'd helped do some interviews for him.

Since the boy had been taken in Eugene but found in the state park, both the US Forest Service and Eugene Police could claim jurisdiction. All hands were on deck. Throughout the day, the Coroner's van showed up, the Crime Scene Investigations Unit showed up, and a raft of uniforms from the US Forest Service and Eugene Police arrived to monitor the crime scene. Unfortunately, it took about two hours before anyone from the NecroFind research team or Harri and Jake had their witness statements taken.

Harri had let the NecroFind team go before she and Jake had just finished up. It was four-thirty in the afternoon, and she was exhausted.

Detective Robinson motioned over to her. Jake smiled at her as he walked by and joined some of the uniforms sitting in the staging section. Everyone from the NecroFind team had gone back to the inn to regroup. No decision had been made about continuing the search, but Harri didn't have her hopes up.

"Thank you so much for waiting as long as you have, Detective Harper," Detective Robinson started.

Harri sat down in the folded chair opposite the older cop. Detective Lewis Robinson was a man in his 50s with ebony skin and a closely cropped head of hair. He had smile lines around his eyes, but his exhaustion showed. His mouth was set in a thin line.

"I'm sorry that we found him like this," Harri said, guessing the older detective had hoped to bring the child home.

"Thank you, Detective Harper."

"Should I go through the last twenty-four hours with you?" Harri asked.

"Yes, why don't we start from there."

Harri recounted how she and Jake had arrived at the Portland airport the day before and driven down to Eugene to speak with Tim Ledeyen.

"Why meet with Tim Ledeyen?"

"He was the last person to see my sister Lauren alive." She explained the circumstances of their visit and the search for her sister's remains.

"This is the same Tim Ledeyen with the missing son?" Detective Robinson asked.

"Yes. We found out about Dan from Molly Ledeyen. Tim was out searching for Dan. I spoke with Detective Gavin French about the disappearance not long after. We'd become friends over the years as he'd taken over Lauren's case with the Eugene PD. I said I would help the family."

"As I understand, he hasn't yet been found?" Detective Robinson asked.

"That's correct."

"And where are you staying?"

"I'm staying at Daniels Inn. I always stay there when I come to search for my missing sister."

"I'm not familiar with that case," he said. "When did she disappear?"

"She disappeared on September 23, 1994. She came here to the Tamolitch Pool trailhead to hike with Tim and her friend Stephanie Lebron. She left the others to go back to the car to get water and was never seen again. The keys to the car had been found at the head of the trail right there," Harri said and pointed to the opening in the forest trail.

"Have you found any evidence that her body might be in this forest?" Detective Robinson asked.

"She vanished without a trace. The only thing that was ever found were the keys," Harri said.

"Your sister went missing here twenty-five years ago. The boy she'd been with had his son go missing the day before you arrived, one day before the anniversary of her disappearance. And now we've found the body of another boy some hundred feet away from the spot she went missing," Detective Robinson said.

"This is all a coincidence, don't you think?" Harri

asked. It was quite a stretch to think the disappearance of her sister, an eighteen-year-old college student from twenty-five years ago, could be connected with a missing sixteen-year-old addicted boy and a thirteen-year-old boy.

"The woods are always a popular place to drop bodies, I suppose," Detective Robinson said. The look he shot the forest made her think he didn't particularly like the outdoors much.

"Not a fan of this forest?"

"My mother told me too many fairytales. The woods are dangerous places and I'm sure there are many bodies still hidden inside of them," he said with a grimace.

"Do you think we'll be able to continue the search for my sister's remains?" she asked.

The detective leaned back and sighed. "Not at this present moment. I don't think he was killed here, but he was dumped right off a popular trail. Somebody wanted him found." He sighed again.

"What is it, Detective?" Harri asked.

"Between one detective to another," he started. "This one's a weird one."

"The clothes?" she asked.

"Yes, the clothes. They're spotless. Clean and pressed. The boy, too. He's been washed. I'm sure you've seen your share of weird cases down in Los Angeles." Detective Robinson's shoulders hunched.

"Did Jake mention he was an FBI profiler?" Harri asked. "He's seen weird ones like this before."

"Yes, he did. I have a call out to Quantico right now." He scratched his head. "All right, thank you, Detective Harper."

"Any idea of a time of death?" Harri asked. She

wasn't sure if he would answer her question, but it was worth asking.

"Looks like forty-eight hours ago. Which means your team are all in the clear once we check out the flight manifests for each of you. Once we get that squared away, I'm hoping we can use NecroFind to help us with the scene. We could use the manpower."

"I'll speak to Dr. Susan about that," Harri said.

"I'm sorry, Detective Harper."

"I'm sorry too, Detective Robinson." She stood up and picked her way back to Jake who was leaning against their rental car.

"This is going to be an ugly one," he said.

"Why?" Harri asked even though she knew the answer already.

"The appearance of the victim's body speaks to a particular pathology. This isn't going to end with one victim."

"I assumed the same. Have you offered your services to Detective Robinson?"

"I wanted to talk to you first. They won't let us search here now."

"I know," Harri said.

She looked helplessly out at the darkening woods, thinking of what Detective Robinson said about the bodies buried within them.

"Have you seen Dan Ledeyen recently?" Jake asked.

"Why?"

"What does he look like? Does he look sixteen?"

Harri bit her lip again thinking back to the meeting she had with Tim last year. Dan had flitted in and out of the kitchen, his bony shoulders poking out of his t-shirt.

"He looked small for his age. He had a slim figure.

Lots of acne. He couldn't be more than five and a half feet tall."

"He looked young for his age then?"

"I don't like what you're getting at," Harri said.

"If Dan Ledeyen isn't drugged up somewhere, then he disappeared soon after Atticus Menlo was dumped. Atticus was missing for eight days. We could be looking at a similar pattern here."

"Thirteen is very different than sixteen when it comes to these kinds of predators, I thought," Harri said.

"If it was an opportunistic grab, and Dan is as small as you say, then it's within the victim profile," Jake said. His face was as drawn and worried as Detective Robinson's was.

"We have a week to find him then," Harri said.

"I hope. When the killer finds out how old Dan really is, we might have a problem."

"Dammit."

The loss of a loved one destroyed lives. Her sister's loss and assumed death killed her mother and sent her father into a dark spiral of alcohol and depression. Tim had confessed how much guilt he'd felt over Lauren's disappearance and Harri knew all too well the grief and panic Tim and Molly had to be going through right now.

"We focus on bringing Dan Ledeyen home. I can pick up my sister's investigation when we find him."

Jake nodded in agreement. "I'll offer my services as a profiling consultant to Detective Robinson. The FBI needs to be invited to help even profile a case and with only one victim, I don't see that they will."

"Do you think he has the budget for that?" Harri asked. She knew how tight budgets were at the LAPD and that most cops weren't fond of outside aid.

"It's always worth a try," Jake said. "The age of the

victim might bolster my prospects of joining the team. No one wants a case like this to drag."

"I won't be able to talk to you about the case then?" Harri asked, knowing there was no way she'd be able to get on a Eugene PD case.

"You keep searching for Dan," Jake said. "I'll keep an eye out for any connection to his disappearance with Atticus' death. If I find one, I'll bring that to Gavin and Detective Robinson and get you to come in to download what you've found. I don't think anyone will mind bringing a kid home whatever the method."

Harri wasn't sure about that but agreed anyway. The body of the boy flashed in her mind again and she turned away from the woods.

The devastation of loss punched a hole in her gut. She remembered the panic and worry; the horrifying nightmares of what Lauren was enduring as Harri and their parents searched for her. She imagined Tim and Molly going through the same thing.

"I'm going to call Tim and tell him our plans."

"I'm off to see Detective Robinson," Jake said.

He squeezed her hand before walking off. She pulled her cellphone out, her hand trembling.

6

DAY 2 - NIGHT

Harri Harper stepped out of the shower into the small steamed-up bathroom. She checked her watch and found she had ten minutes to get ready. The search party, including NecroFind, Harri, and Jake, decided to meet over dinner to talk next steps. It would be a short conversation.

Unfortunately, Harri saw no other options besides canceling the search. Detective Robinson must have already spoken with Dr. Susan about helping at the crime scene. It's what she would do if she'd been in Robinson's position. Harri hoped Dr. Susan would be willing to share whatever information she could with them tonight. Her disappointment at ending the search after a year of pleading her case with NecroFind was tempered by her focus on finding Dan Ledeyen.

She wiped the steam from the bathroom mirror and smoothed down her dark hair. She leaned in and peered at herself. Her green eyes stared back at her and the purple smudges she'd had for the last month had grown deeper. Her face registered the horror of the crime scene. Every line and crease appeared deeper to her. She'd aged ten years in a day. Harri bet some of the others at the scene today would show similar symptoms of shock.

Her mind wandered to Jake and the now familiar feeling of butterflies in her stomach awakened at the thought of him. She didn't understand this new reaction she was having towards him. Maybe it was the more natural reaction of seeing death and wanting to experience life in some way.

Harri pushed the butterflies away. This was not the time or place. She refocused on Dan Ledeyen's disappearance as she rushed to get ready. The boy in the woods was not her case. Eugene PD would not let her get anywhere near it. Her mission was to bring Dan home in one piece, wherever he was.

She finished drying off and put on new black blouse and black slacks. She checked herself again in the mirror. Good enough. Harri grabbed her purse and her door key. She locked the door behind her and headed downstairs.

Jake waited at the entrance of the dining hall for her. Her breath caught when she saw him. His skin glistened from the dampness of his recent shower. His brown hair curled at the top of his white shirt and his rolled-up sleeves exposed his deeply bronzed forearms.

Harri's heart skipped a beat. Jake Tepesky had grown into a handsome man. Jake smiled and Harri's world stopped for a moment.

Get a grip, Harri thought. She smiled back.

"Thank god for hot showers," she said.

"Indeed," he said.

His eyes flicked down her body and Harri blushed.

"Have you seen any of the NecroFind team inside?" she asked.

Jake's eyes met hers. "They're already inside saving us seats," he said.

Harri nodded and followed him into the dining room. Four tables were pushed together to form a large square fitting eleven chairs, two of which were empty. The NecroFind team was eating appetizers and drinking wine, beer, and water. Harri waved at Dr. Susan and they made their way over to the large table.

"Thank you for saving us a seat," Harri said.

"Of course," Dr. Susan patted the seat next to her. "I'm so sorry, Harri. I know how much this search meant to you," she said as Harri and Jake sat down.

"You've heard then," Harri said.

Dr. Susan nodded.

"Detective Robinson said that it would be at least a week, if not two, for the crime scene techs to comb for more evidence. In my professional opinion, the victim's body was dumped there and not killed there. Either way, it's an active crime scene," Harri said.

"Which we won't have access to," Dr. Susan said.

"Right. We'll have to wait for another time," Harri said.

A waiter came over and distributed dinner menus. Harri took the offered menu and focused on what she should put in her stomach. She wasn't hungry but needed to eat. A wave of exhaustion crashed into her and her vision blurred. Protein. She needed protein.

She found a burger under the dinner section. That would do. She placed the menu back down again and turned to the rest of the table.

"The way you work differs so much from what I've seen before. It was fascinating to watch," she said. "I'm sorry to have to tell you that we won't be able to go back to the site for the rest of the week."

"We found a body," Doug said. "It's not the one we were looking for, but we were successful."

"Many times, we don't find bodies," said Robbie the botanist.

"Your success rate is pretty high, though," Harri said.

"We have successes. But we've had more failures. When we first started, not finding a body was a big disappointment. We're scientists, though and we've used those failures to hone the processes for the next crime scene," Dr. Susan said.

"I have to tell you though, finding the boy like that startled me," Doug said.

"Have you come across a lot of bodies in a similar state?" Harri asked.

"I've seen my share of bodies. I'm military and served overseas. This one was different," Doug said.

"How so?" Harri asked.

"One of the crime scene tech guys asked me to take a closer look at his hair," Robbie the botanist cut in.

"For plant matter in his hair?" Harri asked.

"Exactly. And you know what was weird?" Robbie asked.

"You didn't find any plant matter," Jake said.

"That's exactly right," Robbie nodded. "There was no debris in his hair. At all. The tech combed his hair in front of me. The body had to be transported in a bag to keep it that clean. His clothes were pristine. They had no grass stains or dirt marks on them."

Robbie hesitated, then crossed his arms. "What I don't get is this. The boy's body was in that forest for over forty-eight hours and no animals scavenged it? That's not normal," Robbie shook his head.

"Did you notice any odor coming from the body?" Jake asked.

"I didn't know animals were so discerning," Harri said.

"That's the thing. They're not," Robbie continued. "That was the first crime scene we've ever been at that animals didn't touch. In all the years we've done this. I don't know what to make of it," Robbie said.

"That's a good point," Harri said. "Could they have gotten the time of disposal wrong then?"

"That's right. Just because he had been dead for forty-eight hours doesn't mean that he couldn't have been dumped until earlier this morning," Jake said.

"I'm sure the detectives and coroner are trying to nail that specific timeline as we speak," Harri said.

"Are you going to be helping on this case?" Dr. Susan asked.

"A friend's son is missing. I'm helping look for him," Harri said.

"I'm consulting with the police on the body we found," Jake added.

Harri hadn't had a chance to speak with Jake about whether Detective Robinson had agreed to bring him on. She shot him a glance.

"He called me right before dinner," Jake explained at her questioning expression.

"You're an active FBI profiler, then?" Dr. Susan asked.

"No. I do private consulting now. Using my profiling skills to assist various jurisdictions," Jake explained.

"I've never heard of profiler consultants," Robbie the botanist commented.

"It's not really a thing. I retired from the FBI last year. Some of my fellow colleagues had private clients and I decided to try my hand at it. I can choose the cases now and that helps my sanity."

"You think there's any connection to this case and your sister's case?" Dr. Susan asked.

"I don't see how there could be," Harri shook her head. "It's a boy, not a girl, and the age is so different that it would be a completely different type of killer profile. Don't you think, Jake?" Harri asked.

"I agree. Woods tend to make particularly good dump sites. I'm thinking this is a strange coincidence."

The waiter came over to take orders and everyone's attention shifted to dinner. Harri glanced over at Jake and he took her hand under the table and squeezed it.

She was so thankful for the reassurance that small gesture made. She blushed and smiled at him again. "Thank you," she mouthed to him.

Jake's dazzling smile made her heart flutter. She always kept her emotions checked, but his closeness and attention to her were making her walls crumble. Warmth spread through her body as the heat of his hand pulsed in her own. She was grateful for his being at her side especially under such harrowing circumstances.

The food was warm and welcomed, and for once Harri ate everything on her plate. The rest of the table enjoyed their dinner. Dr. Susan surprised Harri by telling her that most of the team was leaving first thing tomorrow morning. When Harri questioned her further, she was surprised to hear that Detective Robinson didn't ask them to help search the woods. It was a foolish mistake on the part of the Eugene PD in her opinion. But it wasn't her case.

The dinner ended and everyone said their goodbyes.

"If you need us again, call. I'll find a way for us to come," Dr. Susan said.

"Thank you for that," Harri said.

Harri noticed Dr. Brand off to the side.

"Have a safe flight, Dr. Susan," Harri said and approached Dr. Brand.

"Would you mind sitting down with me and talking about the Willamette Forest?" Harri asked.

"What do you want to know?"

"I'm not sure yet. Can I call you?"

Dr. Brand handed Harri her business card. "Sure. I'll help in any way I can."

Harri waved goodbye to the NecroFind team and found herself alone with Jake.

"Want to grab some tea? I'm not ready for sleep yet," Jake said.

"Same," Harri agreed.

Jake went over to talk to the remaining waiter as Harri stepped through the double doors to her right into the sitting room. Jake soon followed her in.

"They'll bring us some tea," he said.

They chose two adjoining comfy chairs in front of a large fireplace and sat down in front of the fire to watch it crackle.

The waiter came in and set the tea service for two down on the small table to Harri's right and left them alone. Once they'd made their teas, Harri and Jake settled into the chairs.

Harri sipped her tea and relished Jake sitting next to her. She enjoyed his closeness after such a terrible day. Crimes involving kids only ever got worse. They took a toll on the detectives investigating them. The world was a cruel place.

"Things didn't go as planned today," Jake said.

"No, they didn't. No one should ever find a child like that. My heart goes out to his parents."

"I agree. Murder is hard. Murder involving kids is unthinkable," he said. "How are you handling the canceled search?"

"Not so great," she said. "I put a lot of work into getting them here."

"Lauren would understand your changing direction like this," he said.

"I know," Harri nodded. Of course, Lauren would have understood. It was a child. Lauren loved children and was good with them.

Harri sighed. "It was a real crappy day."

"These kinds of cases are one of the reasons why I retired from the FBI."

"Yet, you offered your help."

"It was the right thing to do," he said.

"They never do get easier," she said.

Jake took her hand in his and squeezed it. "I'm glad I was able to be here with you. To support you, at least."

"Thank you. It's so strange. I don't know how I did it alone before. All those years, coming up here. Going over everything again and again. I don't know where I got the energy to keep at it."

He nodded. "Yes, you do," he murmured.

Harri looked over at him. She did know where the drive for the truth came from.

Lauren.

If roles were reversed, Lauren would never stop until she found the truth, until she found her sister. Harri would never stop, either.

Tim and Molly Ledeyen crashed into her thoughts. She knew what they were going through. She remembered it.

"If we can help bring Dan Ledeyen home then this

was all worth it. Once he's found, I'll go back to looking for Lauren."

"The NecroFind team was a brilliant move on your part," Jake said.

"It was. And we did find a body."

He squeezed her hand again and she noticed he had leaned closer to her. Close enough for her to feel his breath on her cheek. She turned her face toward his.

Their lips touched, gentle at first then more insistent. Harri closed her eyes and let the warmth spread throughout her whole body.

The timing was awful. This was not the time or the place or the circumstances, but his lips were so soft and gentle. He pulled her closer to him and she let him.

Her lips parted slightly, and his tongue flicked inside.

This was good. Their kiss was pleasure and sadness and all the things she missed by constantly being alone. By being haunted by Lauren and her parent's ghosts.

After a moment, they separated, their faces inches away from each other.

"I wanted to do this since I saw you in Mitzie's car," he smiled.

"I'm sure you did," she said.

"Well, maybe at that dinner," he said. He went in for another kiss, but she stopped him.

"I don't want this to start here. Whatever this might be. Let's wait until we get back to Los Angeles and on more neutral ground. This place is haunted," she said.

He smiled, his eyes were warm and inviting.

"I can wait," he said.

"Hopefully, I can. I'll be remembering that kiss for a while," she teased.

"Is that right?" he asked, his eyes on her lips.

"We should get to sleep. We both have an early morning."

"If you're sure," he said.

Harri nodded. "I'm sure."

He stood up and held out his hand for her. She took it and he pulled her up to standing. He embraced her and stole one last kiss. It took all Harri's control to push him away.

"That's not fair," she said.

"No, it's not," he said. "I couldn't help myself."

7

DAY 2 - NIGHT

Richard Miller sat down with his beer in front of the television. Claire liked watching Rachel Maddow at six every night and he was okay with that. Maddow was one of the better news hosts.

"Dad, I'm thirsty," Richie whined from the doorway of his room. Claire had put him to bed, but it typically took about an hour of him asking for food, drink, or another story before he finally fell asleep.

"I gave you a drink in your thermos," Claire said, irritation creeping into her voice. "Drink that and don't leave your room." Claire's patience was wearing thin.

"Mom, can you tell me another story?" Richie asked in his little-boy-voice.

Claire threw down the magazine she had been reading and stomped towards the room. Richard decided to leave them to their arguments and check out the hockey game playing on the local station.

He flicked over to Channel 7. A newsflash interrupted the commercial for Cheerios.

"The body of a young boy has been found in the

Willamette Forest today. This is just breaking..." The newscaster droned.

Richard clicked off the TV.

His body broke out in a cold sweat. He thought back to the phone call from yesterday and the man whispering it was starting again.

And now this.

A boy in the woods, in the Willamette Woods?

Richard stood up and paced back and forth. How could it be? Did they know where he was? Did they know his new name?

What if they came after him or his boy?

Who could he call to ask?

Richard didn't have any of the names from the old days. He had tried to exorcise that whole time away. He did everything he could think of to purge it all from his memory. He didn't want to be a part of that group of boys anymore. He had moved on. He was an adult with a family of his own.

They found the boy in the woods.

They had never been so sloppy.

If it wasn't them, then who could it be? And why would he end up in that same forest? Could it be such a coincidence?

Claire came out of the room and saw the look on his face.

"What happened, honey?"

"Nothing," he said.

She didn't know about any of that. He had kept that away, locked up, hidden in a box in a tiny part of his brain. She would not be sullied by that filth. Neither would his son.

"I gotta go for a drive," he said.

"Now?"

"It's not that late. Do you need anything at the grocery store?" Richard asked.

"You can get some milk," she said, unsure. "I'm not sure I want you driving in the state you're in."

"I'll be fine. I just need some fresh air."

He grabbed the car keys from the end table and stalked out of the house. He didn't want to have a panic attack in front of her.

Richard never wanted to have her see how damaged he truly was. He threw himself into the car and started it. The radio blared and he yanked the knob down to zero. He couldn't breathe.

He rolled down all the windows. The cold night air was soothing to his burning throat.

They had found the boy in the Willamette Woods.

"Have you ever been camping before?" Rich asked Bobby excitedly. They had arrived at the parking lot adjacent to the thick dark forest as dusk was fading into night. Rich had seen the sign for Willamette State Park about fifteen minutes ago as the van entered a heavily wooded area.

"No, I haven't. I guess we'll be hiking there in the dark?" Bobby said. He grinned.

"So cool," Rich whispered. He didn't want to give away just how excited he was for these two weeks. He'd had a hell of a time convincing Donna his foster mom to let him come and had pleaded with her for days until she'd finally relented.

A small van with seven seats had picked them up at the Y, an hour ago. He, Bobby, Jim, Nelson, and George had clambered into the van with their backpacks and sleeping bags. Jim, one of the foster kids that always came to the Y with bruises, only had a small satchel. Rich figured that he's snuck away instead of asking permission from his foster dad. Jim eyed the driver of the bus warily.

Rich wondered why since Mark, the driver and one of the counselors that had been handing out flyers for this camp, had been nothing but nice.

"All right, boys. Grab all your things. I have flashlights to hand out for everyone who doesn't have one. We'll need to hike for about twenty minutes to get to the lake," Mark said.

The boys all obeyed and jumped out of the van. Mark and Jim were the last ones out. Mark pulled out a plastic bag from his backpack and opened it up.

"Go ahead, grab one. We don't want you to get lost in the woods now do we?" Mark asked and grinned.

Rich stepped up and stuck his hand in the bag. His fingers found a round plastic surface and he pulled a flashlight out. He flicked it on and put it right under his chin.

"I'm going to get you…arrrggh," he joked. Bobby giggled and pushed his way past him for his own flashlight. After the three other boys were outfitted with their own flashlights, the group started towards the woods, Mark taking the lead.

Rich inhaled the smell of pine and smiled. His heart jumped in anticipation of the fun they would have. Swimming in the lake, canoeing, talking with the guys over a campfire. He'd pinch himself to see if this wasn't a dream if Bobby hadn't shoved him a second ago almost making him trip. The pain in his ankle told him he was wide awake. The smile on his face grew as Mark stepped into the woods. This was going to be life-changing; he knew it. He'd been in foster care most of his young life and none of his foster parents had paid much attention to him. They made sure he was clothed and fed and made it to school. That was it. But to have fun in the woods and experience something like camping? No way.

It hadn't even been a possibility until Bobby brought the brochure to him. He could hear Bobby whistling behind him.

• • •

Richard shook the memory off with a scowl. They had all been so naïve. It pained him to remember his excitement. He slammed the wheel with his palm. He had to talk to his old friend. Discover what was really going on. Go back to the horrifying summer that had nearly destroyed his life.

8

DAY 3 - SATURDAY, SEPTEMBER 29, 2018

Harri Harper pulled away from the curb and took one last look at Jake Tepesky's receding back as he entered the Eugene PD station. He'd been called in to give a preliminary profile for the detectives working the Atticus Menlo case.

While he was working that case, Harri would be diving into Dan Ledeyen's life by way of his friends. And for that, she needed to know who they were. She hoped that Tim and Molly were knowledgeable as to who he'd been spending time with.

Her drive to Tim's house took about fifteen minutes from the city center. When she pulled in front of the house, she noticed that both cars were in the drive. She'd thought of calling them to make sure they would be home, but Harri and Jake left so early she wasn't sure if calling at seven in the morning would be such a great idea. So, she hadn't. She pulled her cellphone out of her bag and called them. Better late than never.

"Good morning, Tim. I was hoping to stop by and speak to you about Dan. I'm sure you've heard there was a boy found in the woods. My search for Lauren's remains has been postponed. I want to do whatever I can to help find Dan."

She hung up the phone and hoped that they would get the message. She took a sip of her coffee and waited for a response.

The warmth of the coffee made her mind go back to last night. There was a little bit more kissing in front of her hotel room door before she finally said good night. She had lain in bed thinking about Jake and Lauren and all those long-ago summers in high school.

Lauren would find it hilarious to find Harri hooking up with her best friend. At least, that's what she hoped. She knew above all else Lauren would want to see her happy, and for some inexplicable reason, Jake Tepesky made her happy.

Her phone buzzed with a text message. Tim Ledeyen had received her phone message.

Tim: Is that you outside?

Harri: Can I come in?

Tim: Yes.

Harri: Coming.

Harri stepped out of the rental car. She hadn't traversed the entire yard before the door opened. Tim and Molly crowded into the doorway watching her progress. They looked exhausted. By the red streaks on Molly's face, Harri could see she was still crying.

"I'm sorry I'm here so early, but I just dropped Jake off at the police station and I wanted to get an early start," she explained.

"We want all the help we can get to find our boy," Tim said. Harri nodded and they let her inside.

"Do you want some coffee?" Tim asked her. Molly was visibly shaking and Harri touched her shoulder.

"I'll do whatever I can to bring him home," she said. Molly nodded.

Tim led Molly back to the living room and gently helped her sit down on the couch. He came back to Harri, his face grim.

"Follow me into the kitchen, I'll make you some coffee," he said.

"Thank you, I'd love another one," she said.

"We've talked with the detective that you put us in touch with, Gavin French," he said.

"Any news?"

"No, not yet. And now of course with this boy found, I know all of Eugene's detectives are all on deck. Dan is going to slip through the cracks," he said, stress and anger filtering in his voice.

"Not if I have anything to do with it. I'm a cop and I know how to find people," she said. Tim cocked his head at her.

Fair enough, she thought.

"No, I haven't found Lauren yet. But in all fairness, I wasn't a cop back then. I am now."

"I wasn't even thinking of that," Tim confessed.

He made the cups of coffee as Harri sat down at the kitchen table and opened a little notebook.

"I need to talk to some of Dan's friends. I know that addiction centers are not going to give me much information. His friends might be of help to us, especially when they realize he's gone missing and might be using again."

"He only had one friend in there. Thomas James. I think he's actually still in there," Tim said.

"Relapse?" Harri asked.

"From what Dan told me he felt that he needed to be there another month to be safe. He felt that he was too vulnerable still to go back into his life."

"And what is the facility called?" she asked.

"It's called the Morning Sunrise Institute," he said.

"Really?" she asked.

"That's what I thought when I first saw the brochures, but it's supposed to be the best in the state."

"Hate to ask you this, but what was Dan addicted to?"

"Opiates."

"Did he start with OxyContin?"

"Yeah," Tim sighed. "One of his friends in middle school was stealing the pills from his grandpa. Got my son hooked when he was twelve years old."

"Someone that young, he doesn't stand a chance against that kind of drug," Harri said.

"Damn right. We're in one of the lawsuits suing the drug company that was selling the opiates here in the state. But it's too late for my son. He's had two relapses, but this time it really seemed like it was going to stick."

"What was the boy's name that got him hooked?" Harri asked.

"Alan. Alan Prentiss. From what I've heard he lives on the street. His parents kicked him out after his third rehab didn't take. He'd been stealing from them again."

It was amazing to Harri to see how deep the opiate epidemic had gone into the schools and how young the kids were starting. The epidemic would take years to overcome. So many lives had been ravaged by greed and the powerful drug.

"What were his usual hangouts when he was using?" Harri asked.

"You mean Dan? He mostly scored downtown. Of course, OxyContin was too expensive for a kid to get. Heroin was much cheaper. He stole from us, but he also told us he'd become a street beggar to pay for a fix."

"What area downtown did he most frequent?" Harri asked. Parents typically had no clue where their kids were scoring. Harri hoped Tim was different.

"Yeah, around Eighth Avenue and High Street. The street changes at night and the homeless come out. I'm sure you'll find Alan Prentiss down there if he hasn't overdosed yet."

"And what about his friends now? Since he's been clean. Does he have a sponsor?" she asked.

Harri knew the sponsor could not tell her any specific details, but he'd be able to give her an idea of Dan's state of mind. He would be a better judge of whether or not Dan has fallen off the wagon.

"His sponsor's name was Harvey Weissberg. He met him at one of the youth shelters in downtown Eugene. I think it was called Cochran. He'd been an addict and had managed to pull his life together."

"Does he still work at the shelter?" Harri asked.

"I think so," he said. "I really thought this time was going to be different. The first time he came back a mess. He was easily excited and hyper. Like he was on uppers or something. It didn't take him long to meet one of his old buddies. He was shooting up within days."

"This time was different?"

"He was calm. Dan stayed away from his old friends. He started studying to pass his GED. He wanted a job. He started talking about a future," Tim said.

He covered his face with his hands and sobbed. Harri

waited silently next to him. There was nothing she could say to help him. She sat for another couple of minutes and waited for him to calm down somewhat. When his sobbing has subsided, Harri spoke again.

"I have everything I need to start piecing together his life in the last two weeks. Thank you, Tim. I'm going to start with the last three days. Where did he go? Who did he meet? If we piece together his movement, we can see who he crossed paths with. Do you have his cell phone?" she asked.

Many parents of addicts made sure that they had full access to their children's phones to make sure that they were staying straight.

"No, we don't have it. He took the phone with him and he had been texting his mother."

"You never put any tracking or spy software on there?" she asked.

Tim Ledeyen sighed and covered his face with his hands before balling his fists and pounding his own knees. "No. I wish we had but we did not."

"Do you think you could call the cell phone company and get the records of the texts of the last month?" She knew that if the father called, they would not have to get special permission.

"I'll call them right away," he said.

Harri stood up and put her arm on his shoulder. "I'll try to talk to all his friends in the next twenty-four hours. I'll call you periodically to let you know how I'm progressing. If you think of anyone else he might have spoken to in the last two weeks, call me. I'll put them on my list," she said.

Tim nodded keeping his face hidden. Harri patted him one more time and left him in the kitchen. As she opened the door, she heard the sobbing begin again.

Harri closed the door gently behind her. This family was breaking into pieces and it hurt her heart to be witness to it. She placed her hand over her chest and folded inward.

Harri pushed back her own memories of the day they discovered Lauren was missing. She couldn't relive what the Ledeyen family was suffering through. The hopelessness and loss and anger and confusion. The emotions she and her parents had gone through when her sister vanished. Through the endless months of searching and watching her parents tear themselves apart with the what-ifs.

It would not happen to this family. Not if she could help it.

Her pace quickened as she moved purposefully towards the car.

Dan Ledeyen was out there. Waiting to be found. She would find him even if she couldn't find her sister.

Harri slid into the car and googled the name of the rehab center on her phone. She plugged the address in and clicked on the directions.

There was still time for this family.

9

DAY 3

Harri Harper drove to the Morning Sunrise Institute on the other side of Eugene. She easily found the address for the Institute as it was one of the premier rehab facilities in the area. Apparently, Thomas James had money. She didn't know how Tim Ledeyen could afford such a place. Parents would move mountains for their kids, she supposed.

The drive stretched on long enough to make Harri wonder how large this rehab facility really was. Her car pulled into a circular drive in a vast expanse of green lawn in front of a massive Tudor mansion. The building itself was five stories high, with a wing to the left and a wing to the right. If Harri didn't know better, she would think that she was in the English countryside. A perfectly manicured garden sat on the right of the mansion while tall hedges peeked out from the left side.

Harri parked the car in one of the visitor spots and sat back. The exclusivity of this place might cause her problems. She'd ask for Thomas James and hope that he'd want to help find his friend. She made her way to the imposing wooden double doors and attempted to pull one of them open. It didn't budge. A disembodied voice crackled from her left.

"May I help you?" the voice asked.

"I'd like to speak with Thomas James, one of your patients. I'm a friend of the family," she said. The lie worked and the door buzzed open. One hurdle jumped.

She stepped into a large octagonal foyer with a white marble floor and pale blue walls. A dark-haired, middle-aged woman sat to the right of a grand staircase in front of a computer on a vintage mahogany table. Harri had never seen a rehab center like this before.

"Is Thomas James available?" Harri asked.

The woman surveyed her.

"You look like a cop," she said in a friendly conversational manner.

"I am a cop. But in Los Angeles. I'm visiting friends here."

"Is Mr. James expecting you?" the woman asked.

"No, he isn't. I'm hoping he'll be available to speak to me about his friend Dan Ledeyen. Dan was a patient here," she said.

"Our residents are not called patients here," the woman corrected her.

"It's an impressive facility," Harri remarked.

"It is. Let me call him and see if he's available to speak to you," the woman said and picked up a black vintage phone. The mid-century vibe extended to the accessories, Harri thought. She bet they would have gotten rid of the computer if they could have.

"Mr. James, there is a woman here to see you. She's here about Dan Ledeyen. Are you available to speak with her?" she asked. She listened, nodding.

"Very good, Mr. James." She put the receiver back on its cradle and turned back to Harri.

"Mr. James will see you in the sitting room. He'll be down in about five minutes. The sitting room is through those double doors." She pointed at doors to Harri's left. "Second door to the left. You can enjoy the view of the gardens while you wait," she added.

"I appreciate your help," Harri smiled and followed the woman's instructions.

The empty sitting room was a large library with overstuffed chairs of different silks and brocades overlooking the green lawn through a wall of French doors.

She had no idea what Thomas James looked like, so she stood off to the side of the doors until a young man in his early 20s came in several minutes later. He had shaggy, shoulder-length blonde hair, pale skin, and the stringy lean look of an addict.

"Are you Thomas James?" she asked him.

"And you are?" he asked.

"My name is Harri Harper. I'm a friend of Dan Ledeyen's parents."

Thomas James pointed at two armchairs in the corner of the room. They didn't speak until they were settled.

"I'm not sure if you've heard, but Dan has disappeared."

Thomas James sat up straighter, his attention fully on her. "He hasn't been found yet?" he asked.

"No. It's been close to forty-eight hours," Harri shook her head. "His family is frantic to find him. I'm a detective up from Los Angeles and an old friend of the family. I'd like to ask you some questions about Dan and his stay here," she said.

"Of course. I'll try to help in any way that I can,"

Thomas James leaned forward a little. "Does his family think he's using again?" he asked.

"That's the first conclusion everyone jumped to," she said. "Except for his parents."

"It's not an unreasonable conclusion," he said.

"His parents don't think it's a relapse. They think he's in trouble."

"Dan was a heroin addict," Thomas James replied. "Relapses happen."

"When was the last time you spoke to Dan?" Harri asked.

"Four or five days ago."

Harri jotted that information down in her notebook. "How did he sound to you?"

"Excited. He mentioned his job interview at Starbucks."

"He told you about that?"

Thomas James nodded and folded his hands. "He felt he was successfully re-entering his life again," he said.

"Was he meeting anyone after?" Harri asked.

Thomas's brown eyes became hooded and he leaned away from her.

Harri noted his odd response. The air between them felt charged, changing the moment she'd asked the question. Thomas gazed out onto the garden grounds.

"I don't think I should be talking to you about this," Thomas said.

He rose to go.

Harri grabbed his arm and pulled him down again.

"Dan is only sixteen-years-old. His family wants to find him before the unthinkable happens. Parents never know their child as well as their friends do," Harri said, keeping her voice calm but insistent.

"That's the truth," he smirked. "Look, Dan told me a

lot of things. Things he was ashamed of doing," he continued as he leaned back into the seat.

"We really need your help," Harri said. She was surprised by the reaction to a question he surely must have expected from the beginning of the conversation. It almost felt like acting. Or rather, overacting.

"I don't know." Thomas turned his face away, focusing back on the garden.

"What if it was you? Needing help? Disappearing? Wouldn't you want your friends helping the people looking for you?"

Thomas shrugged his shoulders, "Addicts are addicts. Maybe, he's better off…"

He didn't say dead but Harri knew that's where he was going.

"You can't believe that," Harri said. "You're in here. Getting better. He did it, too. He wanted a future."

Thomas turned back to her, his pupils dilated, his face cold. Harri didn't know how to read his expression. She leaned back in her seat and waited. She'd pushed and guilted. Ball was in his court. Harri watched him carefully.

She had an idea of what he would tell her. She doubted addicts up here differed greatly from the ones down in Los Angeles. Kids who needed to score drugs fell prey to predators and pedophiles. There were a lot of ways a kid could make money using the only thing they had: their body.

"He let men take pictures of him," Thomas whispered.

Harri didn't change position but wrote that in her notes. She didn't want to spook him. "Photographs or video?" she asked.

"He said both," Thomas said.

"Did he mention names? Was this organized or random men?" she asked.

"He ran out of the pills he was getting from his friend at school," Thomas said, instead of answering her question.

"OxyContin?"

"Yeah. A friend's grandfather had it prescribed, but when he died, they switched to heroin."

"Did he mention names?"

"Well, I mean this wasn't a very in-depth conversation we had, okay? But he did mention two names of guys he got money from."

"And those were?"

"Blue and Peanut."

The names dampened Harri's excitement. Of course, they would use nicknames.

"He didn't mention their real names?"

"No. Don't know if he even knew their real names."

"Did he say what they looked like?

"No. He didn't really want to talk about them at all, honestly. He kinda clamped up after that. I told him he should go talk to one of the counselors here because that was abuse. He did and I think he was making progress."

"Would you have any idea where he could've gone to score again?" she asked.

"The only place I know of is downtown Eugene. That's where all the kids hang out, turn tricks, and have easy access to dealers. The whole scene is just a couple of blocks around the YMCA down there. If you walk around down there you won't be able to miss it," he said.

"Do you believe Dan relapsed?"

Thomas James sighed and spread his arms with his palms open. "He's an addict."

Harri chewed on her lip, thinking of her next line of questioning. She worried if she brought up his reaction when she asked who Dan was meeting after his interview, Thomas James would shut down. At the same time, she didn't think he had much more to tell her. She plunged ahead.

"I noticed you reacted when I asked if Dan had a meeting after his interview?"

"I don't know what you're talking about. I've been clean sixty-five days, but that doesn't mean I don't get twitchy sometimes."

"Fair enough." Harri doubted that was it but let it go. He would not tell her anything else. "Thank you for speaking with me. And about Dan's secret, I'll be as discreet as I can be with that information."

Thomas James pursed his lips and nodded.

"Just find him. He's only a kid. He didn't deserve any of this," he said and stood up.

Harri followed his lead.

"No one does," Harri said.

Thomas stared back at her with blank eyes. The man unnerved her.

"I'll see myself out," Harri said and walked towards the doors.

Thomas stayed frozen in front of the French doors, looking back out on the garden.

Harri followed the route out of the facility, waving a last good-bye to the receptionist before returning to her car.

She unlocked the rental car's door with shaking hands. Her lack of sleep coupled with the adrenaline of having a direction in Dan's case made her jumpy.

She bet that Blue and Peanut probably had a file on

them somewhere. It wasn't information she could take to the police, though. Not yet at least. If these two men preyed on Dan, then they preyed on other boys, too. She was sure if she found the area where Dan operated, she'd find other boys who know Blue and Peanut.

Maybe, even know their real names.

Her phone beeped with a text message. She rummaged through her bag until she found her cell phone and pulled it out. It was Jake.

Jake: I'm done. You?

Harri: Just finished. I can swing by and get you?

Jake: Waiting outside.

Harri: Be there in 15.

Throwing her bag into the car, Harri sat in the driver's seat and turned on the engine. Something was nagging at Harri and she didn't want to entirely acknowledge it. Was it that much of a coincidence that a thirteen-year-old boy was found in the woods and then a sixteen-year-old boy that looked like a thirteen-year-old boy went missing around the same twenty-four-hour period of time? In a small city like Eugene?

She drove the car down the drive as theories swirled in her mind. She didn't have enough to connect the two cases yet. But a child pornography ring could be responsible for both.

Harri turned onto the main artery leading into Eugene sort of remembering where the police station was. She programmed the address into her phone and the British voice she chose told her to take a right.

There wasn't enough evidence to link the cases. Pornographers wouldn't want to lose such a valuable asset as a boy they'd already groomed. Better that the cases weren't linked. The last thing Harri wanted was to find Dan in those woods.

10

DAY 3

Harri pulled up to the Eugene Police Department and Jake Tepesky hopped into the car. He flashed her a smile as she drove away.

"What did you find out?" he asked, bypassing any pleasantries.

"You first. I've seen that look on your face before. Must be something big?"

"You know I can't tell you that," Jake smiled.

"What about if I ask questions and you say yes or no?" Jake gave her a look. "What about a nod or shake of the head."

He nodded and Harri couldn't help but grin.

"Was Atticus redressed before being left in the woods?"

Jake nodded.

"Was he manually strangled?"

Jake nodded again.

Harri had gotten close enough to the body to see there were no tell-tale lines on the boy's neck although bruising was evident.

"Did they find any biological material on his body?"

Jake shook his head no.

Interesting. That meant he'd been washed, just as they initially thought.

"Anywhere? Even in his privates?"

Jake shook his head no again.

"So, he'd been fully washed."

Jake nodded.

"Do you have enough for a profile?"

"The more information I can get the better, but it's a start," Jake said.

"Have they been able to pinpoint time-of-death?"

"They're close."

"Do you think Dan's case is connected to Atticus' case?" Harri asked, sneaking a peek to see his reaction.

He cocked his head at her. "It hadn't occurred to me. Why would you ask that? Does this have anything to do with what you were going to tell me? And where are we going?" he asked. "I was hoping for some food. I'm starving."

"I'm sure we can find food where we are going. I spoke with Tim this morning and he gave me the names of Dan's friends and sponsor. His sponsor works at the Cochran Youth Shelter downtown close to where the kids score around here."

"Definitely will need to eat before going to interview someone," he said.

"Maybe you can start yelping restaurants while I drive," she suggested.

She glanced down at her phone to check the directions and took a right turn.

"What are the police doing right now?" she asked.

"What's the first thing you'd do if a child was found dead?"

"Bring in all the local sex offenders in the area to see if anyone was involved," Harri said.

"Exactly," Jake said. "Where did you go after speaking with Tim?"

"I spoke with a Thomas James. He was Dan's buddy in rehab."

"And he talked to you?" he asked, surprised.

"I'm persuasive when I need to be," she flashed him a smile.

She'd pushed Thomas James to talk and was glad she had. She recounted what he told her about Dan and the lengths he went to for his drugs.

"Doesn't necessarily need to be an organized crew," Jake said.

"There would need to be some sort of distribution hub, though. Wouldn't there?"

"You have the dark web for that. All you need is an internet connection," Jake said.

"Blue and Peanut could be two small tentacles here in Eugene that connect into a bigger network online," Harri said.

She'd never worked those kinds of cases before. All she knew came from tidbits she'd heard from her colleagues on the special crimes squad and the news.

"We have to assume Blue and Peanut hung around downtown near the Cochran Youth Shelter," Jake said.

"That was my thinking, too. Some of the kids down there might know exactly what their names are."

"Did you get any sort of description from him?" Jake asked.

"No. He said that Dan refused to talk much after the original admission."

"That's unfortunate."

"Could Atticus have crossed people like this?" Harri

glanced at Jake. "Are there more missing boys from the streets that we don't know about?"

"I'll talk to Detective French about that," Jake said.

"The police might not know about it yet. Eugene isn't that big of a city and I know the homeless population has exploded in recent years. They might not be able to parse if any boys are missing from that population," Harri said.

They were getting close to the center of Eugene by her calculations. "Found anything on yelp?" she asked, unsure of where to park.

"How about we just go to Subway? It's a couple of streets over," he said.

"Fancy," Harri quipped.

"I'm hungry and I'm not finding much else down here."

When Harri saw the Subway sign, she pulled into a metered parking space. She checked her phone to see where the Cochran Youth Shelter was compared to the Subway. It was only two blocks.

"We can walk over after lunch. The shelter is only a couple of blocks away."

"Perfect," Jake said.

After finishing their sandwiches at Subway, Harri and Jake walked the two blocks to the youth shelter where Mr. Weissberg worked. Harri wanted to take Jake's hand in her own to feel his warmth.

Thoughts of her sister kept surfacing while they were at Subway. Even though she'd been to Eugene before, she'd often thought of what kind of life Lauren had led in those three weeks she'd spent here.

Had Lauren gone downtown to check the place out?

Had Lauren and her friends wandered around taking in the sights, or maybe tried to get into one of the bars with fake IDs? This was the place she had come to with so much hope and instead, her life ended.

And here Harri was walking along the same streets her sister might have explored. But Harri wasn't searching for her. Instead, she looked for another lost soul, the son of one of Lauren's first friends in this city so new to her.

The absurdity of the situation did not escape Harri. Fingers wrapped around her own and when she looked down, she saw Jake's hand wrapped around hers.

Her heart skipped.

Jake needed comfort, too. Cases involving youth took a toll on the investigators working them. No one wanted to be working the murder of a thirteen-year-old. Or be looking for a missing sixteen-year-old and then wondering what other children were out there waiting to be found or waiting to be discovered missing.

"Are you seeing something on my face?" she asked.

"I am. Were you thinking of Lauren?" he asked.

"I wondered if these streets looked much different to her when she first came here all those years ago," she said.

"I've had similar thoughts. I barely remember anything from the last time I was here."

"Was it that fall that she disappeared?"

Jake nodded and frowned.

"It's a fog in a distant dream that I never wanted to remember. And now, with my eyes wide open and being here with you…while working a horrifying murder case… I have to ask myself if I've taken on a little too much."

"What if you excused yourself from the case?"

He shook his head. "I can't do that."

They didn't speak for several moments until Jake finally smiled.

"I'm only writing the profile anyway. I have you here to anchor me." He squeezed her hand. "Would you have become a cop if she hadn't disappeared?" he asked.

"No," Harri shook her head. "I wanted to go study physics. Maybe get a Ph.D., be a college professor," Harri said.

"I wanted to be a doctor," Jake flashed another smile. "I'd always wanted to be one. A pediatrician, in fact. I dreamed of having my own practice and watching kids grow up. Being part of a family in that way.

He sighed again. "Instead, I see the worst that humanity has to offer. I would've never joined the FBI if Lauren hadn't gone missing."

Harri clutched Jake's hand tightly. He was her lifeline right now.

"But we are here, aren't we?" Harri observed.

"We are. And we can try to bring these kids home before something happens to them," he said.

Harri nodded. They had reached their destination.

"Kids?" she asked as she noticed his turn of phrase. "Are you agreeing with me that more boys have gone missing?"

"It's the fantasy aspect of the case that has me worried. This isn't this killer's first rodeo. He didn't make any mistakes and his fantasy is too-well developed," Jake said.

"You're coming to this interview with me, right?" she asked.

"Isn't that why I'm here?" he teased.

Their joviality was forced, but they'd left their mood behind. It was time to focus on the work ahead.

After going through check-in and getting a bead on where Dr. Weissberg was located, Harri and Jake found themselves in a locker room off a small gym. The lockers hadn't been refurbished in the last thirty or so years. They made their way past grated lockers that ran along each side, green paint chipping.

There was a bench in the middle of the lockers and that's where they found Dr. Weissberg. A bespectacled man in his late 40s with a full beard and balding, he wore a hooded sweatshirt and jeans and was surprisingly fit for his nebbish look.

"Dr. Weissberg?" Harri stepped forward. "My name is Harriet Harper, and this is Jake Tepesky. We've been helping Dan Ledeyen's parents Tim and Molly search for him," Harri said.

Dr. Weissberg gestured for them to join him on the bench.

"Call me George. I don't have an office, or I would bring you there. No one should bother us here for at least another half hour. We can talk here if you're okay with that," he said.

"Thank you," Harri said as she and Jake sat next to him. "Tim and Molly spoke very highly of you and said how instrumental you've been in keeping Dan clean this go around."

She hoped that gave him enough juice to want to talk with them.

"Tim and Molly are really great," Dr. Weissberg nodded. "They've done so much for Dan. I wondered why he hadn't been around in the last few days. I've been out for the last two days with a stomach bug. We were supposed to meet today at ten in the morning, but he never showed."

Dr. Weissberg hesitated. Harri felt Jake shift behind

her and she was grateful once again just for his presence, to know that he was nearby.

"I called Tim and he told me what had happened," Dr. Weissberg continued. "As a sponsor, I'm not supposed to break confidence but whatever I can do to find Dan, I'm here."

"When was the last time you saw Dan?" Harri asked.

"I saw him about four days ago. At lunchtime. He was excited because he'd been doing very well in his GED studies and was even looking for a job. He'd gotten his first interview at a Starbucks and, considering his Juvie record, that was a minor miracle," Dr. Weissberg said.

"Juvie record?" Harri asked. She was surprised Tim hadn't mentioned that detail.

"Dan fed his habit by burglarizing cars," Dr. Weissberg nodded. "He'd been caught and sent to a juvenile detention center. That was around the same time he went to his first rehab."

"Were there any other ways he got money?" Harri asked.

It was as good of an opportunity as any to see if she could corroborate the information that Thomas James had given her earlier that morning.

Dr. Weissberg cocked his head at her. "What are you asking me, Detective?"

"Tim told you I was a detective?" Harri asked.

"That's right. You're a close friend from Los Angeles?" he asked.

"You could say that," she said. "Did Dan ever talk about tricking?"

"No," Dr. Weissberg shook his head. "He did once tell me that he'd break into anyone's house before he would do that," he said.

Harri bit her lip and looked back at Jake.

"What about selling pictures of himself?" she asked.

The question was blunt and didn't come out as nuanced as she would have liked, but by the look on Dr. Weissberg's face about the tricking, something felt off. Dr. Weissberg furrowed his brow and he looked as confused as she was.

"I'm a sponsor, not a therapist. So, I'm sure I didn't hear all his deepest darkest secrets," Dr. Weissberg said carefully. "I spoke to him about getting counseling because I was worried that could be the case. I've sponsored other boys who sold themselves for heroin. He was adamant he'd never done that, nor would he. Nothing ever sexual, he said. He'd rather boost cars. Are you thinking child porn?"

"Yes," Harri nodded. "I've interviewed some friends and they mentioned that as a possibility."

Dr. Weissberg shook his head and held up his hand, stopping her before she could go further.

"I've worked at this facility for going on thirty years now. I've seen kids come and go, and you're right. Many of them do end up doing whatever they have to so they can score. I didn't see that with Dan."

"Was he open about his breaking and entering?" Jake asked.

"He didn't hide it at all. He was ashamed of it and he didn't want to slide back into that."

"Did you ever ask if he'd been abused?" Harri asked.

"I did ask," Dr. Weissberg nodded. "And he was adamant that he wasn't. He was incredibly good at breaking into cars. You wouldn't believe how much stuff you can get in a car and hawk on the streets for dope."

Harri sat and watched him. Dr. Weissberg genuinely believed this.

"Did Dan ever burglar houses?" Jake asked.

"Some of the boys that he ran with did," Dr. Weissberg nodded. "But he always felt houses were too high-profile. That he'd get sent to serious jail if he started doing homes. Cars were his jam. Dan had all sorts of gadgets to get a car door open. He told me once he could hit thirty cars in one night. He roamed all around the city," he said.

Dan wouldn't need to have his picture taken if he had cash flow. From what Dr. Weissberg was saying, he had the money for drugs.

"Do you know who some of his fences were?" Jake asked.

"He used the pawnshop on Eleventh Avenue. It's a couple of blocks away from here. The guy there is a real sleaze and will take anything he can get, no questions asked."

"Got a name," Harri asked.

"Ask for Ruben."

Harri wrote the address and name in her notebook. She didn't believe Dr. Weissberg was lying to her. If he wasn't, and Dan had told him the truth, then why did Thomas James lie to her?

"Have you heard any of the other kids here talk about Dan? Seen him recently?" Harri asked.

"I've asked around since I got off the phone with Tim. No one has seen him all week," Dr. Weissberg replied.

Harri asked if he had any other friends they could talk to, but Dr. Weissberg said that he'd mainly kept to himself. Having exhausted the questions she had, they thanked him for his time and left. Jake and Harri stayed silent until they'd walked back to the car.

Jake broke the silence. "That was unexpected."

"Addicts lie, don't they? The question is, why would he specifically lie about that?" Harri asked.

"Hopefully, you can ask him next."

"We need to corroborate George Weissberg's account with this pawn shop," Harri said and waved her notebook at him.

"Weissberg said it wasn't too far away from here," Jake said and yelped the pawnshop. It was three blocks away. They fed the meter and walked in that direction.

"This boy came in here hocking goods, correct?" Harri asked the grizzled old man sitting behind the bulletproof glass.

"I can't say where any of that stuff came from, but he was in here every day with it," Ruben said.

"How much did he usually get for his haul?" Jake asked.

The guy was friendly to people who looked like law enforcement. This never happened in Los Angeles. When they had explained to him that Dan was missing and they didn't care at all about any stolen goods, he had warmed up quite a bit. He was a real talker.

"It ranged between fifty to a hundred fifty bucks each time he came in. He had a lot of good stuff, expensive stuff. He had an eye for it," the old man said.

Harri had heard enough.

"Thanks for speaking with us," Jake said. He'd come to the same realization.

"I hope you find him. He was a nice kid," the old man said.

"We're doing our best," Harri said.

She and Jake said their good-byes and left.

"Sounds like Dan's rehab friend lied to you."

"Sure does," Harri said. She replayed her interview from this morning in her mind as they walked back to the car. He'd been acting odd. Like he was acting. With what they had found out from Weissberg, Thomas James' odd behavior made some sense. The bigger question is why had he lied? What goal could be achieved by them believing Dan turned tricks?

11

DAY 3 - NIGHT

Richard Miller stood on the side of the road, freezing his balls off. He had gotten the phone call about half an hour ago to meet at this specific corner.

His old stomping ground.

He had lived in a foster home just a couple of blocks away. This block was where it had all begun. That time of his life he couldn't fathom to even remember but came constantly in his nightmares. He looked up and down the empty street.

Bobby had told him he'd meet him here at midnight and it was already thirty minutes past. Had it been a mistake to come out here?

When he saw the news about the dead boy and the potential for other missing kids, he'd wanted to call Bobby immediately. Bobby had beat him to it. What did surprise him was how insistent he was to meet up. Bobby rarely wanted to see other people.

• • •

"Don't look at me," Bobby hissed as he curled himself into a small ball on his bunk. Rich had tried talking to him after he'd gotten back from his own particular nightmare, but Bobby had refused to speak. Instead, he'd curled up on his bunk and cried.

Rich wondered if Mark and Paul had hurt Bobby instead of just taking pictures of him. Bobby was the smallest boy in the group and looked young. Rich figured that those men liked that.

They'd been so excited to come here. The initial hike through the dark woods with flashlights had been thrilling and scary. That had been two nights ago. When the boys got on the island, they were quickly initiated into what they were really there for, however.

Rich climbed onto the top bunk and let his tears fall where they may. He should have known better. Luck didn't bless kids like him and Bobby. They were easy pickings and they had fallen for the dream hook, line, and sinker. Now, they had to find a way to survive long enough to escape this hellhole. He had to keep Bobby's spirits up because Rich doubted he'd be able to get out of this alone.

Richard yanked his mind back from the past and peered up and down the street. He didn't like this. He felt too exposed. Could this be some sort of trap?

Richard looked both ways again. He needed to get back to his car. This had been a bad idea. He'd parked three blocks away, wanting no evidence he had been on this block.

His car was near a park he'd gone to with his son. The thought of his son made him want to leave. To get back to his home life. His clean life. The innocent life he had always dreamed about and somehow created for himself.

He put his hoodie up and walked quickly back to where he had parked.

The screeching of tires behind him told him to run. Instinct kicked in immediately. He ran towards the park, checking behind to see if this was really happening.

It was.

A red sedan sped towards him. His legs pounded the pavement as he sprinted. Richard knew he could not outrun a car, but he could use the narrow alleyway coming up to escape it.

He peeked again. The car had closed a lot of distance and was only thirty feet away. He pushed himself to his limit. Adrenaline rushed through his body and his breath became short gasps.

His heart felt like it would fly out of his chest.

He couldn't die.

After all that he had been through, he would not die.

Flashes of his son and his wife filled his head and propelled him forward. Just as he felt the car's bumper against the back of his legs, he veered into the narrow alleyway. The car's brakes ground behind him.

He had to get into the park. His pursuer would have to follow him there on foot.

Richard ran down the narrow alley and took a right towards the park. His car was on a side street and wasn't accessible from where he was. He would hide out amongst the trees.

He crashed onto the grass and fell into the dirt. He struggled back up, looking behind him.

There was no sign of the car, but that didn't matter. Richard couldn't have whoever was trying to kill him see where he was going.

He clambered back up and kept sprinting until he felt the darkness of the trees around him.

Only then did he stop running.

He held onto a tree and sobbed softly for the boy he had been, sobbed for the man he was now, and sobbed for how much he wanted to live.

To live for his son and his wife.

After what felt like an eternity, he finally breathed slowly without the gasping sobs shaking his body.

Bobby had set him up, he thought.

Bobby was the only one who knew where they would meet. He didn't know anybody else from the old life.

Only Bobby.

And Bobby had betrayed him.

Bobby tried to kill him.

Rage exploded in his chest and he pressed down hard on his wildly beating heart. He would not be that lost scared kid anymore. He would be a man and fight.

He would bring them all down.

12

DAY 3 - NIGHT

Harri and Jake grabbed dinner at a local diner, discussing the next steps after their interview with Dr. Weissberg and Ruben, the grizzled pawn shop owner. Harri had also called the Morning Sunrise Institute to speak with Thomas James, but no one answered the phone.

She'd been surprised by her inability to reach a rehab institution after-hours. Although, she'd never encountered a rehab that presented itself as Morning Sunrise had. Sure, she'd visited the ultra-expensive rehabs in Malibu during a past investigation, yet somehow the Morning Sunrise Institute was another type of place altogether.

They'd agreed to call on Thomas James tomorrow morning when the place opened. The rest of the night was about finding more of Dan's friends and acquaintances while he'd been on the streets.

The homeless population of Eugene came out of hiding after the office workers left the main downtown area. It was the same in Los Angeles and Harri and Jake timed their approach to coincide with the early part of the evening.

Harri flashed a photo of Dan Ledeyen to anyone who made eye contact with them. They'd found some people who recognized him, but they couldn't give much information past that.

"There's a 7-Eleven on that corner," Harri said. "Back in Los Angeles, the side walls of 7-Elevens are a great hangout spot."

"After you," Jake said.

They crossed the street and walked to the left side of the bright building. Three boys huddled against the wall sitting on various sleeping bags. Each boy was under his own dirty blanket.

"Hey guys, can we ask you some questions?" Harri said in her friendliest voice.

The oldest looking boy passed a beer can to the boy on his right.

"You look like a cop," the oldest looking boy said. Dark greasy hair fell into his eyes and his acne-pocked skin stretched over his cheekbones. His boney arms stuck out of his dirty white t-shirt, revealing old and fresh track marks.

"We aren't here in any official capacity. You don't have to talk to us if you don't want to," Jake said.

"Go away then," the same boy said.

"You look like you could use some food," Harri tried.

"Food we got. What we need is money," the boy sitting to the right of acne boy said.

"How about we chat and see if maybe the information you give us is worthy of some remuneration," Jake proposed.

All three boys laughed and snickered. One whispered "Remuneration".

Harri didn't want to feed these boys' habits, but they had struck out with other groups completely. It was getting later in the night and areas like these became rowdy and dangerous as the drugs kicked in.

The youngest-looking boy, sitting to the left of acne boy, looked like he was coming off something. He had long blonde hair and could be easily mistaken for a girl.

"What do you want to know," the talkative boy asked.

"What's your name?" Harri asked.

"Manny," the boy said. "That's Gus," he said pointing to the oldest looking boy with acne and dark hair. "And that's Chuck over there." He pointed to the long-haired blonde boy. "He's coming down right now, so I don't know how much use he'll be," he said.

Harri pulled out the photo of Dan taken a month ago.

"Do you know who this is?" she asked.

"Yeah, that's Dan," Manny said. "He's not on the streets anymore, though."

"Have you seen him recently?" Harri asked.

"Nah. He got clean," Gus said in a voice filled with menace. "He has parents who love him."

"He hang out with you guys?" Jake asked.

"Sometimes," Manny said. "He and his buddy Alan boosted shit from cars in the neighborhood."

He licked his lips and looked at Harri's purse. He'd tell them whatever they wanted for a little cash because his need was overwhelming him.

Harri watched Manny watch her. They had about five to ten minutes more before these boys shut down.

"Has Alan been around here recently? Where does he usually hang?" Harri asked.

"You don't know much lady, do you?" Gus said and took a swig of beer. His eyes showed a feral gleam.

"That's why we're here, talking to you," Harri said. "Tell us what we don't know."

Gus squinted up to her, appraising her.

"Why you lookin'?"

"Dan's gone missing. We're working with his parents to find him," Jake interjected.

Gus turned to Manny then to Chuck. Something unsaid passed between them.

"What you mean by missing?" Manny asked.

"He missing like Atticus?" Chuck asked.

His eyes were glassy and wide. He appeared terrified.

"I thought they found Atticus in the woods," Gus said.

Harri and Jake shot each other a glance.

"You knew Atticus?" Jake asked.

"Yeah, Chuck you knew him, didn't you?" Manny asked.

Chuck nodded his head. His eyes were glazed but he looked more aware since they first arrived.

"Atticus wasn't using, was he?" Jake asked.

"Nah. He was just someone I knew in school. When I went," Chuck said in a voice that was small and scratchy. His need emanated from him.

"Had you seen Atticus recently?" Jake asked.

Chuck shook his head no.

"One of Dan's friends told us about some men he might know. They went by Blue and Peanut," Harri said.

Manny and Gus looked at each other.

"What do you want to know about Blue and Peanut?" Gus asked.

His voice cracked with something Harri couldn't quite place. Maybe he'd been one of their victims too?

"Do you know their real names? What kind of car they drive?" Jake asked.

Gus shook his head no but Harri didn't entirely believe him.

Manny shot glances to both his friends and peered up at Jake. He was accessing how much he should tell him. Harri was sure of it.

"What do you know, Manny?" Harri asked.

"You're looking for some real predators. Ones that like boys a little young," Manny said.

His body had tensed, and he leaned away from the dirty wall. Harri couldn't see his hands, but she saw some movement underneath the sleeping bag that betrayed his nervousness. She felt Jake tense next to her. He was watching him, too.

"We're looking to speak to Blue and Peanut," Jake said. "Do you know their real names? That kind of information we'd really appreciate. Monetarily, of course."

"I know a name," Chuck the blonde-haired boy said. "He used to come around our school a lot. And when I got down here, I saw him trolling all our usual areas. I haven't gone with him, but some have."

He spit some phlegm out next to him.

Harri stayed silent to let him finish. Chuck's eyes flickered with pain and need. His green eyes flashed and were overly bright.

"His name's Chris Becker. He drives a fancy car. I think it might be a Beemer, maybe a Mercedes. But I think it's a Beemer. His daddy's rich," Chuck said.

"Oh, I know that guy," Manny said. "The guy in the fancy white car. He drives down Ninth Street a lot."

"Does he pick up boys?" Harri asked.

"I've seen boys get into his car," Gus said.

The anger had seeped out of his voice. Now he sounded needy and anxious.

"Did you ever see Dan or Atticus go with this man?" Harri asked.

"He drove by Milbourne. Atticus always walked home from school. And he was a pretty boy too," Chuck said.

Harri's chest constricted in pain. These boys broke her heart. She wanted to gather them up and take them home. She wanted to feed them and wash them and help them get clean.

That wasn't her job, though.

Dan was still missing.

They could try to steer the boys towards the Cochran Youth Shelter even though she doubted they'd go. The drugs had such a hold on them.

"You boys know about the Cochran Youth Shelter on 11th? They have a lot of services." She faded off when Gus put up a hand to stop her talking.

"You can't help us, lady. We told you what you want. Just give us some money so we can have a fix for the night. That's as good as we're gonna get," he said.

Jake nodded.

He opened his wallet and gave each boy twenty bucks.

"Be careful, guys," Jake warned. "Don't get into any unfamiliar cars for the next couple weeks. Looks like there's someone who likes killing boys your age."

The three boys rolled their eyes and Manny saluted Jake.

"I'm serious," Jake warned.

All the boys nodded, but Harri knew they would do whatever was necessary to keep from getting sick. At this point in their addiction, it was all about keeping the sickness away. The ecstasy of those first few times was long gone.

"Thank you for speaking with us," she said.

They left the boys to their beers and desperation and walked back across the street.

Jake was already dialing the police.

"I need to speak to Detective Robinson," he said. He listened and Harri could hear Detective Robinson's voice on the other line.

"Detective Robinson, I've been speaking to kids downtown searching for Dan Ledeyen."

He stopped to listen.

"I understand that. We've found something, though."

He listened again.

"That's right. Dan Ledeyen still hasn't been found."

Harri gestured to ask Jake what was being said but he waved her off.

"We've come across the name of a man who has been seen at Milbourne, Atticus's high school and we've been told he comes down here to pick up boys. Might want to have him checked out. His name is Chris Becker, and he drives a white BMW."

The voice on the other end lowered his decibel.

"You're welcome." Jake clicked off.

"That didn't sound like it went well," Harri remarked.

"Detective Robinson has been interviewing all known pedophiles in the area. Chris Becker is on that list."

He checked the time.

"It's close to one in the morning. We should get some sleep and start this back up again tomorrow. Go see Thomas James," he said.

Harri agreed, but she also knew this was prime time for anyone on the streets to be interviewed. Many homeless had places to crash during the day and nighttime was when all the business was done. She didn't want to stop asking for Dan until they got closer to discovering who Blue or Peanut was.

"We should go talk to those boys about Alan Prentiss," Harri said.

"You think you'll be able to get any more information out of them?" Jake asked. He sounded doubtful.

"They were the first kids willing to speak with us," she said.

"You know some of the others knew the boys as well, but didn't want to get involved," Jake said.

Harri knew he was right, but there was really no way to push people into talking in her capacity as an out-of-state cop.

They crossed the street one more time.

"Manny, you mentioned Alan Prentiss. Do you know him well?" Harri asked as soon as they were within earshot of the huddled trio.

"I know him as well as anybody else," Manny said.

"You know where he hangs out?" Harri asked.

"He hangs out with us," Chuck said. "We haven't seen him all day, though."

"He was supposed to meet us, but he never showed," said Manny.

"He's probably passed out somewhere," Chuck said.

"Is that not normal for him?" Jake asked.

"Nah," Gus said. "Alan was all broken up when Dan left for rehab. They were thick as thieves going out on their nightly runs together."

"Alan's gotten into some bad business since Dan got clean," Chuck added.

"So, who's the one with the breaking-into-cars skills?" Harri asked.

"That's all Dan. Alan had to find other ways to get money," Chuck said.

"The kind of ways that Blue and Peanut offered?" Jake asked.

Chuck nodded.

"He hasn't been seen in twenty-four hours either?" she asked.

"Nah," Gus said. "Guess not."

"Did Alan have any contact with Dan while he was in rehab?" Jake asked.

"Alan was pissed at Dan," Gus explained. "Dan cleaning up messed up Alan's whole gig."

Manny nodded. "He needs his buddy at his side to get that cash," he said.

"Thank you," Harri said.

Jake gave them more money and walked with Harri back to their car. She was grateful to feel his hand protectively on her lower back as they walked.

They found the car and proceeded to get in.

"Dan's disappearance is somehow involved with Atticus," Harri said as she buckled up her seatbelt.

"Agreed. What are we looking at here?"

"Atticus fits into this somehow. He doesn't sound like a kid who's fallen into drugs like the others. Could he have been vulnerable in a different way?"

Jake started up the car. "I don't like the fact that Alan Prentiss has gone missing now, too. The time between abductions has shortened. Our killer's devolving. Needing his fix faster."

Harri nodded. "Atticus went missing a week ago. His body was found four days later. Dan disappeared forty-eight hours ago and now Alan has been missing for what seems to be twenty-four hours. That's an astonishing level of escalation."

"You think they'd let us in to see Thomas James tonight?" Jake asked.

"No way. We wouldn't get through the gate. The place opens up at eight."

"Six hours of sleep. I'll take that," Jake said as he pulled onto the highway.

The motion of the car made Harri's eyes droop.

"I can't keep my eyes open. Will you be okay if I close them until we get back to the Inn?"

"I have too much adrenaline in me. Go ahead and rest. I'll get us there," Jake said.

His voice slipped away as Harri surrendered to sleep.

13

DAY 4 – SUNDAY, SEPTEMBER 30, 2018 - MORNING

After a quick breakfast of bagels and coffee, Jake and Harri drove to the Morning Sunrise Institute and arrived at 7:59 AM, one minute before the Institute opened for guests.

Dew clung to the grass making it sparkle like diamonds. Birds trilled in the distance and Harri wished she could just breathe in the fresh air and relax. This was not possible, of course, but Harri tried to take even a second to appreciate the beauty of her surroundings.

This case was getting to her and she needed the momentary reprieve. Glancing at Jake, she wondered if he needed some release himself.

"You slept well last night?" she asked.

Jake shook his head.

"Couldn't stop thinking about those three boys at the 7-Eleven. How do you come back and restart your life after being like that? I kept thinking of what we could do to make their night better for them. I felt like crap about giving them money for drugs. They're just so young and we used them."

Harri nodded. Her thoughts ran similar to his this morning. They hadn't really offered to give them shelter for the night or drive them to one of the numerous homeless shelters that had sprung up all around Eugene.

They couldn't change anything about the way they'd handled it now. Harri vowed to do things differently the next time they were in a similar situation.

"Let's focus on Thomas James. That's at least something we can control," Harri said.

"You're absolutely right," Jake said. "We save one boy at a time." His jaw clenched as he said that.

She squeezed his hand and stepped out of the car. She groaned as every part of her body ached. She joined Jake as they walked over to the front door, their footsteps crunching on the gravel.

"This place is impressive," Jake remarked.

"Wait until you get inside," she said.

She pressed the button to announce their presence. The buzzer sounded and the door clicked open.

"Thank you for letting us in," Harri said to the same dark-haired severe-looking woman sitting at the desk that she'd encountered before. "I called several times last night around nine. You don't answer the phone after hours?"

"That's correct. Our main line is closed down at six when I'm off duty. Relatives of our residents have access to a private number to check in on their guests if needed."

"I was calling to see if I could speak with Thomas James again. I have some more questions for him," she said.

"Unfortunately, that's not possible," the woman said.

"Why not?" Harri asked, rather bluntly.

"Because he's no longer with us," the woman said.

Harri's mouth fell open. That was not what she was expecting to hear.

Jake took over.

"Are you saying he's dead?" Jake asked.

"No. Nothing like that," the receptionist flustered. "He just up and left."

"He can do that?" Harri asked.

"He was here voluntarily," the receptionist shrugged. "If a patient here feels like he no longer needs our help to stay sober, then he can leave. He's not a prisoner here."

"When did he decide to leave?" Jake asked.

The receptionist shook her head. "You know I can't give out that kind of private information," she said.

"But that's not private is it?" Jake countered.

"I can't tell you that," the receptionist's voice turned sharp. "You can infer whatever you like, but we do have rules around here about our residents."

"Thank you for your help," Harri said to the receptionist just as sharply as Jake's cell buzzed in his pocket.

He pulled the phone out and showed Harri the screen. It was Detective Robinson. They crossed the foyer and stepped outside. Only then did Jake answer the phone.

"Hey Detective Robinson, what can I do for you?"

He listened while his brow furrowed.

"You picked him up?" he asked. "Uh-huh, uh-huh."

They walked back to the car and this time Harri got behind the wheel as Jake sat into the passenger seat, phone pressed against his ear. She didn't start the car.

"Thank you so much for informing me, Detective Robinson. I'll come in later today to check out the report as it stands to add to my profile," he said.

The call lasted a bit longer. Jake said good-bye and hung up.

"Did they find someone?" Harri asked.

"They picked up Chris Becker first thing."

"This is first thing," Harri said, checking the time. It was only 8:15.

"He said early morning hours so I'm thinking they must've busted the guy's door down last night after I gave them his name."

"Did he confess or something?" Harri asked.

"They held him in a drunk tank overnight to keep him from skipping out. They questioned him this morning, but he lawyered up pretty quickly. From what Detective Robinson said his lawyer was one of the most expensive in town. His father is that tech tycoon that started the online delivery company, DriveDash. He must be a billionaire at this point," Jake said.

"Great." Wealth gave perps a lot of latitude.

"Becker refused to answer any questions and then the lawyer came, and they didn't have anything to charge him with. They wanted an alibi for when Atticus went missing and he came up with some excuse of being with one of his father's employees. They're checking it out now, but obviously, that's flimsy at best."

"He's out then?" Harri asked.

"That's what Detective Robinson said."

"We can find Chris Becker's address and go talk to him ourselves," Harri said.

"That's not a good idea. We'd be seriously stepping on Eugene PD's toes if we do that," Jake said.

"Yeah, but we're the ones that got his name."

"Harri, why are you even considering it?" Jake sounded surprised.

"Because we're still looking for Dan," she said. "It's three days he's been missing now. Becker could be the individual Dan met with after his Starbucks interview. Do you know anyone who could get us his address?"

"You can't be seriously asking me that."

"No, I guess I'm not."

They sat in silence for a moment. Harri looked over at Jake. He looked out the window back at the lush gardens of the Morning Sunrise Institute. Harri kept her gaze on him until he turned back to face her.

"Okay," Jake acquiesced. "If we can find Becker's address ourselves, then we can go. But I'm not calling in any favors. That's crossing a lot of lines."

Harri acknowledged the twinge of guilt she felt for asking in the first place. She wasn't acting like a professional, but she couldn't let Becker slip away.

"All right then. Let's go back to the Inn and regroup. Do some internet sleuthing," Harri said and started up the car.

She drove them back to the Inn and left Jake nursing another cup of coffee as she went upstairs. Harri booted up her laptop and searched for Chris Becker's address. She found a lot of information on his father the senior Becker, but little was listed about Chris.

After half an hour of research, she hit pay dirt. Chris Becker had an arrest record for indecent exposure. A local paper had listed his name and address in conjunction with his misdemeanor citation. Was that what put him on the sex offenders list or was there something more? Something sealed?

Another question to ask Chris Becker when they saw him.

Harri scooped up her laptop and ran down the stairs to find Jake.

"I found an address. It's a couple of years old but we can check and see if it's still good," she said.

"How did you find it?" Jake asked.

"A newspaper listed his address while reporting local crime."

"What did he do?"

"Indecent exposure. Do you think that would put him on the sex offenders list?"

"I think he'd have to do something more for that," Jake said as they left the Inn.

Harri read out the address near downtown Eugene. Jake plugged it into his phone, and they drove off. Jake didn't look especially happy at the turn of events, but Harri did her best to ignore him.

Something stirred in her belly. It was her gut telling them they were finally on the right track.

14

DAY 4 - AFTERNOON

Harri and Jake's drive to Chris Becker's apartment took them about half an hour. They'd arrived in downtown Eugene with Jake's stomach growling. It was close to lunchtime and his voracious appetite just couldn't wait.

Harri parked in front of a coffeeshop advertising sandwiches. The place was what Harri would call nondescript. They both ate egg salad sandwiches in relative silence. Harri watched Jake. His mood seemed better. The laughter was still in his eyes when they met hers across the table.

Harri couldn't sit still, her excitement at speaking with Chris Becker overflowing. Jake took his time, occasionally telling Harri to stop fidgeting. They both had another cup of coffee before walking the three blocks to Becker's last known address.

The walk was good for Harri as the added caffeine made her jumpy. As they rounded the corner of Becker's street, Harri spoke up.

"I'm going to take the lead on this."

"Why?" Jake asked. His tone said he wasn't in full agreement.

"Because I'm trying to keep you out of trouble. Detective Robinson told you about Becker and his release."

"You didn't think of that before we decided on speaking with him?"

"It's the first lead we've gotten that could be real," she confessed. "I almost wish you weren't working as their profiler."

"But I am. And you are a cop. And we are definitely stepping out of bounds."

"We're looking for Dan. If Eugene PD let Becker go, I see him as free game." She was pushing it, she knew.

"Maybe you shouldn't come in with me. It'll give you plausible deniability," she said.

Jake shook his head. "We're doing this together," he said.

"I'm a cop, Jake. You don't need to protect me," she said.

"I understand that, but I'm going in with you."

She shrugged not wanting to get into an argument with him, especially out in the open on their subject's street.

"We're here," she said, checking her phone.

Chris Becker's apartment was in a 1970s era apartment building with peeling paint and sagging windows. His apartment was on the first floor. Harri was surprised the place wasn't any nicer. For his father being so wealthy, Becker certainly didn't seem to be getting much benefit from it.

"The newspaper listed his apartment as number four," Harri said.

They arrived at an orange door with the number four hanging tilted in the middle of it.

Harri knocked three times.

There was no answer.

Harri knocked again.

"He's not home. We should go," Jake said.

Harri's curiosity got the best of her and she peered into the window she assumed was his living room.

Feet peeked out from behind the worn couch.

"We have a body," Harri said.

Jake pulled out his phone. "I'm calling it in."

Harri touched his arm.

"We don't know if he's dead. If the cops come, we're completely out of this. We'll never get into that apartment."

"What are you saying, Harri? We're breaking down the door to see if he's still alive?" Jake asked.

"My thoughts exactly."

"I thought that was only something you see in the movies," he said.

"Maybe. We're citizens here, though. They can arrest us for breaking and entering." She sounded a lot surer than she felt.

She took a deep breath. How far was she willing to take this? She had no jurisdiction here. Eugene PD didn't consider her a cop, but a citizen,

With that, she grasped the handle and twisted it.

Surprisingly, it was open. She looked at Jake who shook his head no and she opened the door.

The coppery smell of blood hit her nostrils. This man was definitely dead.

She stepped inside the small living room and looked around. There was a stained brown sofa against the wall with a flatscreen TV affixed to the opposing wall.

A broken coffee table littered with beer, cigarettes,

magazines, and an old piece of pizza took up most of the floor.

There was a door to a bathroom and another door leading into a small hallway. She looked over at the body and saw a gun a couple of feet away.

"There's a gun here." She checked the victim without touching him. "I see a shot to the head."

"Suicide?"

"I think it's supposed to look like a suicide."

"Supposed to?"

"Something isn't right about it, though." Harri stood in the middle of the room. She'd investigated suicides before. She couldn't figure out what was wrong, but something was.

"Harri."

Jake's tone stopped her short. She'd been headed down the hall to check out the rest of the apartment when he'd said her name.

His face was pale. He'd found something.

He licked his lips and pointed at something on the battered desk that was sitting against the wall near the window.

She walked over to him and looked down at where he was pointing. An old group photo in a wooden frame sat on the edge of the desk. The photo was of a young woman and eight boys.

Harri's mouth fell open.

Her sister Lauren's face stared back at her.

Her sister looked scared and exhausted. None of the boys were smiling either.

The photo was taken in a wooded area with a sign peeking out from behind the group. Harri made out the letters C-A-M and what could be a P hidden by one of the boy's heads.

"Are you seeing this?" Harri asked.

Jake nodded.

He went to touch it, but Harri stopped him. "We can't touch it."

Jake blanched. "It's her."

"Take a photo. I'll point it out when the cops come. You get out of here and I'll call it in."

"I'm staying here with you," Jake said.

His jaw clenched and the look in his eyes was different from any she'd ever seen before. His eyes were cold and completely closed off to her.

"We need to make sure you can stay on this case," Jake said.

Harri sensed he'd gone into a clinical mode, purely professional.

She shook her head. "Becker was connected somehow to Lauren's disappearance. With his possible connection to Atticus Menlo, you will be off this case if Robinson finds you here. I'm gonna take the heat for this. Go," she said.

They stood across from each other. Jake had his hands on his hips and Harri's arms were crossed. They stared each other down for a few moments, not aggressively, just each of them holding their stance. Jake didn't back down.

Then a thought struck Harri.

"Why didn't they leave the cops watching over him?" Harri asked. "That's what we would have done."

"You're right," Jake said. "Why didn't he have any watchers?"

The energy in the room lifted.

"Are you leaving?"

"No."

"You aren't making a smart decision," Harri said as she dialed Detective Gavin French.

"Detective French speaking," he answered.

"Hi, French," Harri said. "It's Harri Harper. I have another body for you."

"What are you talking about," Gavin said.

"I'm at Chris Becker's apartment. He was one of the leads I got while searching for Dan Ledeyen. When I arrived at his apartment, I saw his feet behind the couch. I thought he might need my help, so I entered. He's dead."

Detective Gavin French didn't respond right away. Harri was about to ask if he was still on the line when he finally spoke.

"I'm on my way," Gavin said.

"Why wasn't anyone watching his apartment?"

"Uniforms were on their way to stake out his place. It took a while to get the paperwork. He left our custody not even two hours ago."

"Is it because his daddy is so rich?" Harri's tone came out a lot angrier than she had expected.

"No, Detective."

Harri noted Gavin's defensive tone.

"We needed to make sure all the I's were dotted, and the T's were crossed. The elder Becker is an enormously powerful man in this state with an army of attorneys," Gavin explained.

"Right. See you soon," Harri said and clicked off.

She turned back to Jake, frustration showing on her face.

"They didn't have anyone on him yet," she said.

"I'm not leaving you here."

"Let's wait for the cops outside," Harri said.

"Leave the photo for them." Jake nodded.

"We don't have to point it out just yet. Let's see if Gavin recognizes my sister," Harri said.

They walked out of the apartment and stayed near the front door. Sirens sounded in the distance.

"Here comes the cavalry," she said.

Jake grimaced. Harri bit her lip as she leaned against the wall, her sister's face seared into her mind.

The investigation into Becker's killing would be a media circus. The pedophile son of a billionaire found dead. Unless it was ruled a suicide. At least another sicko was off the streets.

She looked back and wondered why she thought that it wasn't a suicide even though the gun was just a little bit away from his hand. It was a coincidence of timing. He was dead two hours after he got out of police custody. What were the chances of that?

Apparently, Chris Becker had an army of attorneys who most likely would've been able to get him off. Why kill himself now?

And then there was the other problem.

If he was Atticus Menlo's killer and he had also taken Dan and Alan Prentiss, then where were the boys?

They sure as hell were not in this apartment.

With Becker dead, the boys would be without food and water. Her stomach clenched. She caught Jake's eye.

How were they going to find Dan now?

15

DAY 4 - AFTERNOON

The Eugene PD came out in full force to meet Harri and Jake at Chris Becker's apartment. Detective Robinson and Detective Gavin French were the first to come up to check out Becker's body followed by a group of uniforms securing the scene.

Detective Robinson was thunderous and Harri could tell he was working hard not to yell at her. Gavin took over and got them into the car and calmed his friend down. At least, that's what it looked like to Harri. Jake and Harri were shuttled back to the station for questioning.

They were put into separate interrogation rooms. Harri had asked for water and had been sitting there for close to two hours before anyone came to speak to her. She was upset they were treating her with so little respect. She was an LAPD detective for god's sake.

At the same time, she had been at the last two crime scenes discovering bodies. Putting herself in their shoes, she could understand why she'd been held there that long.

"Sorry about the wait," Gavin said as he came in.

Harri was glad for that egg salad sandwich she'd had with Jake earlier. Her stomach grumbled in response. It was past three o'clock in the afternoon and she hadn't even had water.

"If I wasn't a cop, I'd be really pissed at you right now," she said.

Gavin cocked his head at her, and his eyes flashed.

"Well, since you are a cop, you should understand why we had to do this."

"Did you see it?" she asked.

"What are you talking about?" Gavin sat down and looked confused.

"The photo on his desk."

Gavin swiped on his phone. Harri leaned over and watched as the photos from the crime scene came and went. He finally scrolled to the photo on Chris Becker's desk.

"You know who that is, right?" she asked.

"I'm not sure…" Gavin said but stopped when he peered closer.

Harri could see he had the image zoomed up close to the picture of her sister and the boys.

"Holy shit," Gavin said. "Is that Lauren Harper?"

"That's right. That's Lauren. And I know for a fact she never went to camp." Harri paused, waiting for Gavin to take in what she was saying.

"Also, the woods look very much like the woods around here. That man had something to do with my sister's disappearance," she said through gritted teeth.

"That's not possible. Chris Becker was only thirty-seven years old. Back then, that would've put him at…"

"Twelve years old. How much you wanna bet he was one of those boys in that picture?" she asked.

"Is that what you were doing there?" Gavin responded.

"I was with Jake interviewing some boys at the 7-Eleven on the Dan Ledeyen case. That's why Jake called Detective Robinson last night with Chris Becker's name," Harri explained.

"We got his name from three boys when we asked them about Dan and his whereabouts in the last week. They knew him from the old days. If you can call two months ago old days."

"They give you his address, too?" Gavin asked.

"I found it online. He'd been arrested for indecent exposure a couple of years ago and the paper listed that address. I was surprised they actually gave it out like that, but I guess if you're a felon then they don't care about privacy," she said.

Gavin wrote that down. "What time did you get there?" Gavin asked.

"We arrived there soon after lunch. I would say around twelve-thirty," she said.

"And then what?" he asked.

"I knocked on the door. When he didn't answer, I checked the window to see if maybe there was somebody inside. That's when I saw the body on the floor," she said.

"And why did you not call the police at that point?" he asked.

"I didn't know he was dead. I was under the assumption he needed help. I checked the door to see if it was open and it was. I walked inside; Jake was right behind me. That's when I saw that he was dead."

"And that's when you called the police?"

"Exactly. As I was leaving, I noticed the photo on his

desk. I knew immediately that was Lauren. I still don't see how she's connected to this."

Harri sat back, still not fully believing this was happening. After all these years of searching for her sister, she'd been shocked to find her connected somehow to the disappearances of boys years later. It still didn't make sense to her.

Apparently, it wasn't making any sense to Gavin either.

"What were the names of the boys you got Chris Becker's name from?" Gavin asked.

"We didn't get last names, but they introduced themselves as Chuck, Manny, and Gus."

"And this was regarding Dan Ledeyen's missing person's case?" he asked.

"That's right."

"Thank you, Detective Harper." He stood up to go.

"I need to pee, Gavin. Are you seriously gonna keep me in here for another couple of hours?"

Gavin turned to her. "You've found two bodies in the three days since you've been here. Robinson is going to want to come in to question you, as well," he said.

"I don't know anything about the Atticus case," she said. "The bloodhound found him. I came here to search for my sister like I do every year. As the cop on her cold case file, you know this because I call you every year. Everything else I've just stumbled onto."

Gavin folded his arms across his chest.

Harri continued. "Could it really be just coincidence that Tim Ledeyen's son was one of the boys that have gone missing? Have you linked the cases together yet?" she asked.

"Which cases?" Gavin asked.

"Dan Ledeyen's disappearance and Atticus Menlo's

death. Oh, and another boy seems to have gone missing. His name is Alan Prentiss. He's an addict like Dan and hung around with all those kids downtown," she added.

"I'll look into that," Gavin said.

"Can I please use the bathroom?" she asked.

Gavin gave her a wry smile and gestured for her to follow him.

"I hope you'd be this sweet to me if I found two dead bodies on your patch," he said as he led her out of the room.

He pointed her to the bathrooms.

"Of course, I would," Harri said even though she knew that sometimes procedure was procedure and if their roles were reversed, he probably would've sat in that same room just as she had for hours.

About an hour later they finally released Jake and Harri on their own recognizance. They had been cleared as mere witnesses and Harri and Jake decided that they would treat themselves to a nice dinner. Jake found a steakhouse in Eugene that had amazing reviews and they both sat down with a glass of wine. Harri could not believe the events of the day.

"Are you still consulting with them?" she asked.

Jake shook his head.

"Nope. I've been relieved of that position, as you said I would be. I did give them all my notes for a profile."

"You're a civilian like me now then," Harri said.

"That's right. No more insider information for us," he said with a wink.

"Well it's not like you were giving anything away anyway," Harri said. "That picture, though."

Her shock had given way to a renewed determination

to discover exactly where that place was. Where Lauren had been held and by whom? She assumed one of the boys had been Chris Becker. She would be calling on Becker's father to get a picture of him.

She also had a phone call out to Dr. Brand, the woman who was an expert on all things Oregonian and supposedly knew the Willamette Forest like the back of her hand. That camp had to be in the forest and Harri would find it.

"I have the photo of the boys," Jake said. "I'm not sure how we're going to identify all of them twenty-five years later," he said.

"Maybe we should start with the missing child database online. What's it called?"

"NamUs," Jake nodded.

"Maybe you can start searching through the database while I beg Becker's dad for childhood photos of him."

"I don't think he'll want to talk to you," Jake said.

"Probably not, but it's worth a shot." Harri sipped her glass of wine. "I also called Dr. Brand while I was waiting for you. I set up a meeting with her first thing tomorrow morning to have her look at the photo. I'm hoping she'll be able to put us in touch with Robbie the botanist."

"Slow down, Harri."

"Why? This is the closest I've gotten to Lauren."

Jake swallowed a bite of steak.

"I just want to make sure you're okay."

"I'm better than okay," Harri said.

Adrenaline coursed through her system. There was a trail. She'd finally found it. The look on Jake's face stopped her.

"What's wrong?"

"I was thinking of the photo."

"And?"

"The trees. The photo looked like it had been taken in the summer."

Harri frowned. Tension coiled in her stomach. The wine in her mouth turned sour.

"Lauren disappeared in the early fall," she said.

"They kept her alive, Harri," Jake said quietly. He let that sink in. "Whoever took her, kept her alive. She must have been a captive for almost a year."

Nausea rushed up into Harri's mouth as the horror of what Jake was saying flooded through her. Kept her alive. Captive. Almost a year.

16

DAY 4 - NIGHT

Harri and Jake only pretended to eat the rest of their dinner. They sat in almost silence. The realization of what Lauren must have gone through in that year quelled any excitement Harri had in finally discovering a solid lead. Jake's face appeared haggard. Harri could only imagine what he must have seen as a profiler. He knew better than anyone what Lauren must have gone through.

They called it an early night. Harri hoped a good night's sleep would prepare them for the big interviews they had planned for the next day.

Harri was ready to ambush the senior Becker at his office in the hopes of getting a photograph of his son at age twelve. If that avenue didn't work, she'd have to troll the internet for any information or photos on the young Chris Becker. She wasn't hopeful she'd find anything because people in the early 90s hadn't been on the internet yet. At least, their photos weren't.

They drove back to the Daniels Inn still without speaking. Harri wasn't interested in making small talk and Jake wasn't either. Theirs was a comfortable silence and Harri was thankful that Jake was with her.

They hugged goodnight at her door and as Harri was about to go in, she turned back to face him.

"Thank you for being here, Jake."

He smiled. "Good night Harri."

"Good night, Jake."

As she closed the door on his smiling face, she knew the smile wasn't genuine. She knew he put it on just for her and that he was smiling through the pain and horror of their discovery. It made her cherish their renewed friendship even more.

Harri threw her phone and purse on the bed and turned towards the bathroom when her phone buzzed with a call. Having no idea who might be calling her at this late hour, Harri rushed to answer it before the caller hung up. Her heart dropped when she saw who it was. Her lieutenant at the Los Angeles Police Department. Violet Howard never called her this late. It couldn't be good news.

"Harri here."

"Harri, it's Violet," her Lieutenant said.

"Is this a friendly call, Violet?"

"What do you think? I can't imagine what you could have done to warrant the phone call I just got from a Detective Robinson at the Eugene PD," Violet said.

Harri was gladdened to hear Violet's tone as frustrated, but not angry.

"I've discovered two dead bodies," Harri said.

"You haven't killed anyone, have you?" Violet asked her dryly.

"Did Detective Robinson imply that I had?"

“He was angry enough.”

"I didn't go looking for them. The only set of remains I’ve been looking for, I still haven’t found," Harri said.

She wasn’t sure she wanted to tell Violet about her searching for Dan Ledeyen. His disappearance was too uncomfortably close to the Atticus Menlo investigation.

"There's no way I could get you to come back down here, is there?" Violet asked.

“It’s my time off, Violet. Are you asking me or telling me to come back to LA?”

Harri knew Violet was a big supporter of hers and that Violet understood how important these yearly visits up to Oregon were for Harri. With everything that she'd uncovered, Harri wasn’t going anywhere.

"I can't make you do anything, darlin'," Violet said. "I'm just giving you a friendly phone call to let you know that you’re ruffling feathers up there. Ruffling somebody enough to have the balls to call one of my bosses down here about you."

Harri's heart dropped for the thousandth time that day. Her stomach was still not doing very well and even though she managed to eat half of her steak at dinner, her stomach had grumbled in protest.

"I finally found a viable lead to what happened to my sister, Violet. After close to ten years of coming up here and looking for her, I finally found something. No one can take me off this path.”

"It could get messy up there for you," Violet said.

“It already has, Vi. But this time I’m bringing my sister home.”

“Watch your step, Harri. You've made some enemies up there," Violet warned.

"What else is new?”

"You got me there," Violet said and the two women said their goodbyes.

Harri clicked off the call and bit her lip as her stomach grumbled with liquid.

She dragged her purse onto the bed and paused.

Had somebody been in her room?

She looked around. Housekeeping had been there, of course. She couldn't shake the feeling. All her senses were firing.

Somebody had been in her room.

This morning, she'd left her computer in the middle of the table. She was sure she had closed her laptop, but now the lid was slightly open as if somebody hadn't closed it all the way.

She frowned and walked over to the laptop. She pulled open the screen and the laptop woke up from sleep.

The internet browser was still on the news article that had given her Chris Becker's apartment address. Had she not shut down the laptop?

What was that sound? Water running. It had to be coming from the room next door. She turned around and stared at the closet. Without making a sound, she tiptoed over to her bed and pulled her service weapon out of her purse.

She pulled the gun out of its holster and undid the safety. With the gun pointed down to the ground, she crossed the room in four steps to the closet door. She stopped in front of it and put her gun at the ready. She swung the door open with her left hand and found herself staring at an empty closet.

"Don't lose it yet, Harri" she said to herself and redid the safety on her gun. She closed the closet door and hesitated.

She should check the bathroom. Just in case. She undid the safety again and walked to the bathroom door.

Harri inhaled and threw the door open.

The bathroom was empty.

The bathtub, however, was quickly filling with water. Harri hadn't showered that morning, so there was no way she'd have left the water on. She put her gun away and reached over to turn off the water.

That's when she saw it.

It was dark and floating in the middle of the bathtub. It looked like seaweed, but she knew it was a clump of hair.

A clump of hair with something shiny attached to it. Harri ran back to the bedroom and grabbed her purse. She pulled out her bag of plastic gloves and her pack of evidence bags. She never went anywhere without either of them for this reason. Harri put the gloves on and peeled one of the bags off.

She returned to the bathroom and plunged her hand into the cold water, grabbing the hair in the process. She pulled the gruesome patch of hair out and put it into an evidence bag. She zipped it closed and only then did she look more closely. She sucked in her breath when she recognized exactly what it was.

Her sister's favorite silver pin: a girl with a ponytail riding on a surfboard.

Harri gulped down her scream and took the bag with the hair and pin into the other room.

Someone had left her a message, but it didn't have the intended effect. They were trying to scare her off. Whoever had been in her room wanted her to leave.

Their message had backfired.

There was no way Harri would leave now. The intruder had confirmed to her that she and Jake were on the right path. The path that would lead them to Lauren. Whoever had been here knew where her sister's body was buried. Harri would find them and Lauren. Of this, she was now sure.

Harri went to her laptop bag and pulled out her fingerprint kit. She dusted both the bathroom doorknob and the knobs on her bathtub with fingerprint powder. A few fingerprints appeared but on closer examination, they appeared to be hers.

She dusted the desk and her laptop and found all the surfaces clean. Except for where she had touched her laptop to open the screen. Every other part of the laptop was wiped clean.

Whoever had been in her room made sure they hadn't left anything to identify them behind.

Now, she had to decide whether to call Detective Gavin French about what she had found. She thought of calling Jake, but then decided she couldn't just yet. He needed sleep. He didn't need a new reminder of the horror Lauren must have gone through.

17

DAY 5 – OCTOBER 1, 2018 - MORNING

Harri arrived at the senior Becker's ten-story office headquarters in the center of Eugene early. She lied about an appointment with Andrew Becker that got her to ride up the elevator to his tenth-floor office. She was halfway there and hoped the rest of her ploy would work.

Jake Tepesky had stayed behind at the Inn to search the NamUs database for boys that had gone missing between the years of 1994-1995. He hoped to match the faces of the boys in the photo with those in the database. If they could connect faces to names, they'd be able to talk to relatives about where the boys had gone that summer.

The elevator opened to the penthouse offices of Andrew Becker. It was showtime. Harri pulled her badge out and readied herself to get access to Andrew Becker by any means possible.

"May I help you?" the young blond secretary asked. If Harri imagined the perfect secretary for a billionaire, this woman would be it. Big round blue eyes and short blonde hair made the perky young woman the picture of innocence and youth. The woman had to be just out of college.

Harri put on her best smile.

"Hi there. I'm here to see Mr. Andrew Becker," Harri said.

"Do you have an appointment?" the secretary asked.

Harri flashed her badge at the woman. "I'd like to talk to him about a case I'm working on."

The woman looked at Harri's badge closer. She was sharp. Harri had to give her that.

"This badge is from Los Angeles. Are you working with the Eugene Police Department?" the secretary asked. Harri knew that Eugene PD had to be all over Andrew Becker regarding his son's death.

"I'm not investigating Chris Becker's suspicious death. Rather, I'm here about a crime that happened about twenty-five years ago to Chris Becker," she explained.

The woman picked up the phone and dialed a number. "I have a detective here to see you from the Los Angeles Police Department about a crime committed twenty-five years ago," she said.

The secretary listened and then nodded. She hung up the phone and turned to Harri.

"Mr. Becker will see you," she said.

Harri stepped back in surprise. She didn't think it would be that easy. Wondering what exactly she was going to find in that office, she nodded and stepped up to the large oak double doors.

She opened the door and stepped into a huge office. A massive desk sat in the middle of the room, a gray-haired mustached man wearing a baseball cap sitting behind it.

"I heard the LAPD was sniffing around my son," Andrew Becker said.

"I'm actually more interested in your son as a victim and not as a perpetrator," Harri said.

That got the old man's attention.

"I'm Detective Harriett Harper with the LAPD," Harri continued.

He waved his hand. "Sit," he demanded.

Harri bristled at the command but obeyed because she needed this man's cooperation.

"What are you talking about Chris being a victim?" he asked.

"Did your son ever go to a camp during the summer of 1995?" she asked as she pulled out her notebook.

"Why?" he asked suspiciously.

"I'm going to be really upfront with you, Mr. Becker. I know that your son was identified as a pedophile for inappropriately touching a fourteen-year-old boy five years ago. He also had a felony charge of indecent exposure."

"My son was a horrible man. What of it?" he asked.

"Many times, and this is not giving your son any sort of excuse, perpetrators were themselves victims. I'm investigating a crime that occurred around 1994-1995. Recent information has come to light about a camp being the center of this investigation. I believe your son might have been there at that time."

"I don't know of any camp my son went to," Andrew Becker said. "I wasn't really around back then because I was building up my business. His mother and I divorced when he was ten and I only had weekend visits with him. Maybe that was part of the problem," he said.

"Would you have a picture of your son when he was that age?" Harri asked.

"Why?"

Harri decided to ask a different question.

"When was the last time you were at your son's apartment?" she asked.

"I haven't spoken to my son in twelve years," Andrew Becker said.

"That's a long time not to speak with your son."

"Let's just say when he got caught, that wasn't the first time. I'd sent him to therapists to get him fixed but he couldn't help himself. I washed my hands of him completely," Andrew Becker shook his head in defeat.

"Then how did he get the high-powered lawyer to bail him out yesterday morning?" Harri asked.

"Oh, I had nothing to do with that," he said. "Like I said – washed my hands of him completely."

Harri sat back surprised. That wasn't an answer she was expecting.

"Do you have a picture of him?"

Andrew Becker scrunched up his nose and opened one of his desk drawers. He shuffled papers around until he found what he was searching for. He pulled the photo out and handed it to Harri.

The photo was of a thirty years younger Andrew with a smiling blonde woman and a ten-year-old boy sandwiched between them. They looked happy.

"Do you mind if I take a photo of this?"

"Sure, fine," he said.

Harri pulled out her phone and took a few pictures of the family photo, zooming in to Chris Becker. She had studied the camp photo all morning and was sure that Andrew Becker's recently deceased son was one of the boys in the photo.

"Is your wife still alive?" Harri asked.

"Ex-wife?"

"Of course. I'm sorry. Is your ex-wife still alive?"

Andrew shook his head. "She died of cancer about four years ago."

Damn, Harri thought. The mother always knew what her kids were up to. "Would you know of anyone else who might have known your son back when he was twelve years old? Someone else I could ask about this camp?"

"Is that where my son got molested?" he asked.

His bluntness made Harri wince. He sounded so cold when he said it.

"That's what I'm looking into right now."

Andrew Becker pushed back in his seat. "When we divorced, it was not amicable. My ex was a vindictive harpy and she cut me completely out of both their lives. I had to go to court to even get the visitation rights for my son. He was at that stage where he didn't want to talk to me. I really can't help you with your inquiry because I stopped knowing my son once the divorce was finalized."

Harri stood up and then looked at him. "Do you think your son committed suicide?" she asked him.

Andrew Becker grimaced.

"A darkness lived in my son. It could have driven him to commit suicide. Or one of his freaks did him in. Either way that wasn't my son anymore," he said.

Harri nodded and said thank you.

She left the office without Andrew saying another word.

His forthrightness had surprised her. Most people wouldn't want to admit they had a son like Chris Becker.

But Andrew Becker didn't seem to have any such compunction and that bothered Harri.

She guessed that the cat was out of the bag with Chris

Becker's convictions and there was nothing left for his father to hide. It was the first well person she knew of that had thrown their family under the bus, though.

She stepped back into the elevator and checked the time. The interview had been shorter than she'd expected. Harri wasn't meeting Dr. Jasmine Brand for another two hours.

Dr. Brand had suggested they meet at a coffee shop about six blocks away from here. Harri decided she'd walk there and spend her time searching NamUs herself to identify more boys as the Chris Becker angle had dead-ended. No one was alive to ask about what he'd done that summer.

Harri walked the six blocks to the coffeeshop and found a rustic style university spot. There were students at most of the tables sitting with their laptops open and working while sipping their java.

Harri nestled into a big armchair after getting her coffee from the barista and fired up her laptop. She needed to find that camp.

18

DAY 5 - AFTERNOON

An hour had passed and Harri Harper hadn't made much progress on the missing kids database. By now, Jake Tepesky had joined her and neither of them had found even one boy that matched the boys in the photo.

Dr. Brand arrived about half an hour after Jake had sat down in a plushy chair. Her dark hair was pulled back in a ponytail and she carried maps and a stack of books.

"Thank you so much for meeting with us, Dr. Brand," Harri said. "May I get you a cup of coffee?"

"I'm too caffeinated as it is but thank you," Dr. Brand said.

"Was the photograph at a high enough resolution for you?" Harri asked. She had emailed Dr. Brand the scanned photograph asking her if Robbie the botanist could identify the trees in the background of the photo to give them an area the camp might have been in.

"It was at a high enough resolution. I sent it off to Robbie and he told me he'd get back to me by end of today," she said. "Meanwhile I've begun a search through records to see if there was anyone granted permission to run a camp in any of the national forests. I'm at the beginning of my search, but I've been able to find three camps that were operating in the early 90s on borrowed land from the National Forest Service," she said.

"Were any of these camps in the Willamette Forest?" Harri asked as she beamed at the woman. She hadn't expected Dr. Brand to work so quickly.

"There were two camps in that forest in the 90s."

"Could this camp be one of those?" Jake asked.

"Not necessarily. I broadened my search to any camps in the 80s. Camps could have been operational in '94 or '95, but the records would likely show the land deal in the 80s. Once the land was released for the deal then the new owner could start building on it."

"Did you see anything in the photo that might indicate where the picture was taken?" Jake asked.

"The trees are pretty standard for Oregon. I'm a geologist, though and this isn't my area of expertise. Even the ground cover is hard to read. I can't really identify the grass, either. Any movement on identifying the kids in this photo?" she asked.

"We're still working on that. We've been searching through missing kids databases and have come up empty."

"If you found the photo, doesn't that mean the boys survived the camp?" Dr. Brand asked.

Harri and Jake discussed that option briefly. Chris Becker had returned home after the camp, clearly emotionally and mentally damaged. The other boys could have, as well.

Where were they now though?

The issue that niggled at her was how come none of those men seemed to have come forward about the abuse they'd suffered as children.

Could that be due to shame? She'd read about the numerous other child abuse scandals within religious and sports organizations. She understood the desire for the victims to forget and try to go on with their lives. She understood the need to be normal.

It bothered her how no one spoke about Lauren. She'd gone on various news programs to talk about Lauren's disappearance. She made sure Lauren wasn't forgotten. Surely, one of them had seen her speak about the case over the years.

"We're hoping Robbie might be able to piece together a general area to narrow our search," Jake said.

His phone buzzed. Jake picked it up and checked who the caller was. He shot Harri a glance. It had to be the police or the FBI.

"Detective Robinson? I'm surprised to be hearing from you."

Both Harri and Dr. Brand fell silent, waiting on Jake to finish.

Jake listened and shook his head at Harri. This didn't sound good. He barely spoke, said goodbye to Detective Robinson, and hung up the call. Jake's lips pursed into a thin line.

"Chris Becker's death has been deemed a suicide," Jake said.

"Seriously?" Harri asked.

"Is that the pedophile that was found in his apartment yesterday?" Dr. Brand asked.

"News gets around fast," Harri remarked.

"It hit the national news last night," Dr. Brand said. "He was Andrew Becker's son," she added conspiratorially. "Big money." She mouthed while raising her eyebrows.

"The FBI is now involved in the case. We'll be meeting with them first thing tomorrow." Jake sighed.

"They must have found photos on his computer," Harri said.

The FBI typically didn't have jurisdiction on murder. What they did have jurisdiction over was interstate commerce and crimes happening across state lines. Apparently, whatever photos the police found showed enough to involve the FBI.

"Is your sister's case connected to this in any way?" Dr. Brand asked carefully.

"It's becoming clear that it is," Harri nodded. "Everything seems to have started at this camp, which is why we need to find it."

"Everything?" Dr. Brand asked.

"Predators preying on young boys," Harri said.

"I see. Let's find this camp then. I have probably another half day's work on researching the area. I'll give you a call when I've located more precise locations of these two camps," Dr. Brand said.

"Will you call us as soon as you have a general location?" Harri asked. "Time is of the essence. We don't know how long Dan has, but we have to assume time is running out."

"The missing boy is at this camp?" Dr. Brand asked. Her eyebrows shot up in surprise.

"That's our working theory," Jake said.

"Have you been following the case?" Harri asked.

"This search was my first with NecroFind. I've been around human remains before but those had been bones. I'd never seen a victim like that. It's thrown me, to be honest. I'd like to help in any way I can though," she said.

"We can use all the help you can give us," Harri said.

"Let's meet back here tomorrow afternoon. If you find anything before then, please give us a call," Jake said.

"Absolutely," Dr. Brand said.

She gathered up her notebook and maps.

"Good luck with the FBI," Dr. Brand said as she shook both their hands.

"We're going to need it," Harri said.

Dr. Brand briefly smiled and weaved her way through the tables to the exit.

Harri picked up her cold coffee and took a sip. She grimaced at the taste and put it down again.

"What does the FBI want from us?" Harri asked.

"Nothing good, I should think," Jake said.

"Can we be positive?"

"Not with the FBI. They have all the information they need from the Eugene PD. If they want to talk to us, it's probably to tell us to beat it."

"Great."

"Nothing we can do about that now," Jake said.

"Dr. Brand works fast," Harri remarked.

"Maybe we'll get a location tonight," Jake said.

"I wouldn't count on that," she said. "Anyway, let's focus on what we have."

"We have lots of theories but no clear evidence. What do we know thus far?" Jake asked.

Harri considered telling him about what she'd found in her room the night before, but for some reason held back. She just couldn't tell him yet. A pang of emotion moved through her. Guilt? Regret? No, it was fear. She was afraid to show him something that could be an actual part of Lauren. Why was she holding onto it? She had to show it to him. She had to turn it over to Detective Gavin French for evidence processing.

A slow realization coursed through her. She couldn't let go of Lauren. She couldn't let anyone else touch what could be the only remains she would ever find of her sister. For now, for just this moment, she had to keep what was left of Lauren to herself.

Jake looked around and saw the coffeeshop had emptied significantly since they first arrived. He leaned in and spoke quietly.

"Let's go through it," he said.

"Dan Ledeyen and Alan Prentiss are missing," Harri said.

"Alan offered himself up to predators for money," Jake added.

"Chris Becker has a connection to both Dan and Alan, and the crew downtown, and to Milbourne High where Atticus Menlo went to school."

"Chris Becker is found dead after being put into police custody. We have a photo of a group of boys surrounding Lauren Harper at a camp. We're thinking the photo must be from the summer of 1995," Jake said.

"Chris Becker is a known pedophile and now the FBI is involved," Harri added. "How much do you want to bet they found a ton of child porn on his computer?"

"Obviously. That could mean Chris was part of a child pornography ring. The question is, could he also be a supplier of these pics?"

"He has a willing population of drug users that he can use," Harri said.

"Why take the boys and kill them then? That brings a whole lot of heat to the network. Scrutiny by the Eugene

PD and the FBI. It doesn't make sense that our killer is part of this network." Jake frowned.

"The man who took Atticus, Dan, and Alan isn't a pedophile?" Harri asked.

"I don't think so," Jake shook his head. "He could be something else entirely."

"Why do you say that?"

"The body of Atticus Menlo showed an advanced fantasy. The clothes, the way he was posed. The killer is telling us a story. We just don't know what it is yet."

"How does this connect with our camp then? If the killer is one of the men who was running it, then that would make him a pedophile which you say he isn't."

"What if it's one of the boys? A survivor, like Chris Becker might have been?"

"He's exposing the pedo ring by killing these boys?" Harri grimaced at that theory. "Why not go to the police?"

"He could be too afraid of authority," Jake said. "He might have tried going to the authorities in the past and it was no use, or maybe he was retraumatized. In the killer's mind, that's simply not an option."

Harri could see the direction he was heading in and could buy that theory.

"I keep going back to the presentation of the body. The killer made no attempt to hide Atticus at all. Why clean him and then place him specifically there? It's almost like some kind of sacrifice or tribute. Maybe the killer was taking Atticus Menlo back to a place of trauma to transform it into a place of peace?"

They sat quietly in thought for a moment.

"How can we use this to move forward?" Harri asked.

"Someone needs to talk about that camp," Jake

answered. "We also dig further into this pedo ring. If the killer is trying to expose it, then he knows about it. Maybe he's on the periphery somehow."

"Speaking of the periphery, let's not forget Thomas James. And we should confirm that Alan Prentiss is, in fact, missing," Harri said.

"Why don't we split the work," Jake suggested. "You go searching for Thomas James and I'll speak with the Prentiss family. I can take a rideshare over there."

"Meet back at the Daniels Inn for dinner?" Harri asked.

"You got it," Jake said.

"Unless you need me to rescue you. I'll pick you up," Harri offered.

Jake winked at her and ordered a car on his phone.

"Call me after you talk to them," Harri said.

"Same to you," Jake said.

Harri nodded.

"We'll find him, Harri," Jake said. "My car's here."

He stood up and squeezed Harri's hand. "Good luck."

"You, too."

Harri watched him get into a waiting black sedan. Her pulse quickened as she opened her laptop. They were getting closer. Narrowing down the possibilities. Harri stopped herself from getting too excited. They still needed to find the camp and Dan Ledeyen. And the elusive Thomas James. Outside of his being the victim like he'd told her Dan had been, Harri still had no idea how he fit into this case. Her gut told her that he did, though.

19

DAY 6 – OCTOBER 2, 2018 - MORNING

Harri and Jake Tepesky sat across from Special Agent Nick McNarin in his Eugene FBI satellite office. They'd been kept waiting for over half an hour after their designated meet time and both of them were in sour moods. Harri hadn't been able to make any headway on finding Thomas James. Jake never met Alan Prentiss's parents. And still no word from Dr. Brand.

Now, Special Agent McNarin was taking his damn time in getting the meeting started. He was a man in his early 50s and not typical of what Harri thought of as a Special Agent. He had a round belly that his white shirt strained against. His attempts at hiding his balding were pathetic and his beady eyes didn't inspire confidence in his intelligence. She doubted this interview would go well. Harri had started to shake her leg to get the jitters out.

"I'm sure you both know that I wanted to see you regarding the Atticus Menlo case. And also, the Chris Becker case," Special Agent McNarin began.

"What would you like to know?" Harri asked.

"Why is the FBI involved? Did you find something on his computer to make this your jurisdiction?" Jake asked, his voice steely and cold.

He sounded like he was about to lose his temper. This would not make for an easy meeting.

"Yes. We've been tracking a pornography ring on the dark web and we were not aware that Chris Becker was one of the providers of said content until you found him dead," Special Agent McNarin shared.

Harri was suspicious of why he was sharing so much with them.

"Chris Becker was providing the photos. How do you know he wasn't just sharing what others had given him?" Harri asked.

"There were personal effects recovered in his dwelling of the boys whose photographs were found on his computer," Special Agent McNarin said bluntly.

"Why are you being so forthcoming? I'm a retired FBI agent and I know information comes with a price? What do you want?"

"I know who you are, Tepesky. I'm giving you this information, so you'll know it's being properly handled."

"And?" Harri asked.

"And therefore, you will have no need to remain here in Eugene." Special Agent McNarin continued.

"Has a task force been established?" Jake asked.

Special Agent McNarin didn't respond.

"Are you assisting Eugene's investigation or taking it over?" Jake continued.

"How long do the two of you plan to be in town?" Special Agent McNarin asked in the same nonchalant manner.

"I'm no longer working on the Atticus Menlo case,"

Jake said. "My partnership with the Eugene PD dissolved several days ago. We're here as private citizens."

"Why did you find Chris Becker then? What did you want from him?" Special Agent McNarin asked.

"We've been helping the parents of a missing boy. He disappeared around the same time that Atticus Menlo's body was found. His case slipped through the cracks." Harri said.

"Detective French mentioned his name to me. I pulled up the case file and the first thing I saw is that he's a heroin addict. What makes you so sure he isn't dead somewhere of an overdose?" the Special Agent asked.

Harri shook her head. "Attitudes like yours are why we're here helping his parents. He deserves to be found."

"We're private citizens," Jake said. "And we don't take orders from you." His testiness was back.

"It wasn't an order as much as a friendly warning. You've both been at two crime scenes in one week," Special Agent McNarin replied. "We're working on a connection between both cases in conjunction with the Eugene PD. We don't need your interference in either investigation."

"We're not leaving until we find Dan Ledeyen," Harri said. "You can let Detective Robinson know that when you talk to him next. We made a promise to his parents and seeing as we're both law enforcement officers, we can use our skills to help someone everybody else seems to think is a lost cause."

"Is that all? Can we go?" Jake asked, rising from his seat.

"Look, no one wants to see either of your careers

damaged in any way by obstructing our investigation," the Special Agent said.

There was no menace in his voice but Harri got the message loud and clear.

"Well, that's just great," Jake said with a smile. "Neither do we."

"We'll follow Dan Ledeyen's disappearance until we find him," Harri said.

"I spoke with your Lieutenant, a Violet Howard," McNarin said.

Harri's stomach dropped but she kept her composure. "I'm on vacation from the department. Why would you call my boss?"

"I like to get all the information I can when I'm working a case," Special Agent McNarin replied, his beady eyes locking on hers.

"We aren't on the case, though," Harri countered. "Nor are we suspects."

"Not yet," Special Agent McNarin replied.

The room fell silent.

"I trust you know how to conduct yourselves in a different city during an ongoing investigation," Special Agent McNarin remarked.

Harri got to her feet. Jake was already headed towards the office door.

"We'll take your warnings under advisement. Have a good day," Harri said.

Jake's jaw set, but he kept his mouth shut. Harri had a feeling that if he did say something, they'd be in a lot more trouble than they were already in. She was grateful for his amazing ability to stay silent when necessary.

Neither of them spoke until they were back in their rental car.

"Do you think they'll put a tail on us?" Harri asked.

"Not yet."

"Give them time. I'm not entirely sure we aren't suspects," Harri said. "I wonder if Detective Robinson called in the FBI?"

"Does it matter?" Jake asked.

Jake pulled the car out of the federal lot and headed back to the Inn.

"I guess not. The photos on Chris Becker's computer must have tipped them off to a bigger operation."

"Spanning different states, I'm sure."

"McNarin didn't inspire much confidence in me to uncover a conspiracy like this," Harri said.

"He's the lead in Eugene but the officers reporting to him will be solid. They'll team up with a computer crimes unit." Jake flashed her a smile "There are good people in the FBI."

"He mentioned nothing about the significance of that photo," Harri argued.

"That one photo loses significance when a huge cache of child porn was uncovered at the same crime scene," Jake said.

"Wouldn't you think Gavin would debrief the FBI on my sister's disappearance and the relevant photo we uncovered?"

"The photo wasn't relevant to the investigation. He might have kept it back."

"If he did, that might have bought us more time."

"Exactly," Jake said.

Harri's anger lifted somewhat and she thanked Gavin silently. Jake pulled onto the freeway and headed towards the Inn.

The sun was still low, and the surrounding forest looked fresh and new. She rolled down the window and the smell of evergreen blasted her nose. She inhaled deeply and imagined once again how much Lauren must have enjoyed these surroundings.

Jake interrupted her reverie. "I wanted to give you an option," he began.

"I have an idea of what you're going to say, and the answer is no," Harri said. She was not giving up on bringing her sister home.

"Harri, your job is in jeopardy. Your boss being called doesn't bode well for job security."

"Are you seriously asking me to go back to Los Angeles?"

"You need to carefully consider what continuing up here will mean," Jake said.

"I have considered it."

"I don't like the amount of heat our being here has generated," he said.

"Are you saying there's a bigger case here?" Harri asked.

"Bigger, but obviously not more important than finding out what really happened to Lauren," Jake said. He sighed deeply. "I'm saying that there are powerful people behind this."

"I can only imagine that's why Detective Robinson called my lieutenant."

"FBI and local police are both all over this. We don't know what their positions are. They're both pursuing their cases, and once it all connects, we could lose track of Lauren again, not to mention Dan Ledeyen." Jake said.

They drove in silence for a moment as Harri took in what Jake was saying.

"Since we're talking about this, I need to say that I don't believe Chris Becker killed himself," Harri said.

"Why?"

"The scene didn't look right."

"What about it didn't look right?" Jake asked.

"I haven't put my finger on it yet. But I keep going back to the way the gun was placed near his hand. I don't know. Also, the timing. Was someone watching us at lunch? Did they know where we were headed?"

Jake nodded. "I don't know about that, but why leave the computer with all the evidence behind? If Becker's killer wanted his activities exposed, why not just take the computer and turn it over to the authorities?"

"Are we seeing conspiracies in everything now?" Harri asked.

"If someone killed him, why didn't they take the computer?" Jake said again.

"Either they wanted those photos found, or this had nothing to do with the porn ring," Harri said as Jake pulled into the drive of the Daniels Inn.

Harri didn't want her job to be in jeopardy. She already had enough problems with the LAPD as it was. This situation would only make her life worse.

But the truth mattered.

The truth needed to be brought into the light and this was the closest that she'd ever been to discovering what happened to her sister. If that meant losing her entire career over it, was she going to take the risk? With her stomach roiling, Harri knew the answer to that.

"You won't stay away from this?" Jake asked.

She turned towards him and found him carefully observing her.

"For the last ten years, I've come here banging my head against every door and lost the trail. There was never an inkling of what happened to her. Now, we have something to go on. If we lose this thread, it could be lost forever. Especially with who Chris Becker really was."

"I feel the same way," Jake nodded with a smile.

"Career be damned. We have to find out what really happened."

"And Dan Ledeyen. Besides his parents, you and I are the only ones looking for him. We're the only ones who care."

"What about this," Jake said. "I'll keep following the lead on the camp and Chris Becker. I can be the point person for Dr. Brand, and you focus on Dan's disappearance. That way I can give you some cover from the Eugene PD and the FBI. Dan's disappearance doesn't seem to be concerning them much."

Harri wasn't sure she wanted to do that. She enjoyed working with Jake and there was a certain amount of protection in having a working partner. It was the reason detectives worked in pairs. Your partner had your back.

At the same time, she understood what he was getting at. Calling Violet was a threat she had received loud and clear.

"Are you sure you're willing to take the heat like that?" she asked.

Jake's lips pursed into a thin line. He reached over and squeezed her hand.

"I can take it. Don't worry about me," he said.

20

DAY 6 - AFTERNOON

Richard Miller tried to look nonchalant as he took another lap by the Cochran Youth Shelter off 11th. The last time Richard had seen Bobby was in this general vicinity. The shelter had been the local YMCA back then.

A kid with blond hair over his eyes came up to him. "Hey, my name's Bobby."

Rich smiled. He'd worried that he didn't know anyone here at the Y and was grateful for Bobby's friendliness. Rich had just moved in with his eighth set of foster parents and these ones were decent enough to send him to the Y for the summer. Rich typically kept to himself, but he was tired of not having any friends. He would try harder to be friendlier.

"Hi. My name's Rich. Is this your first day?"

"Yeah. We missed a week though. It looks like everyone's paired off already," he said. They walked into the gym together and saw the different groups of kids already at play.

"We can play together. Do you play hoops?" Rich asked. Bobby smiled grew wide.

"I do now."

Bobby had been so open and eager to make friends back then. That all changed after some bullies targeted Rich and Bobby and they fought back. Bobby had been kicked out for throwing a punch at one of the older boys.

Richard remembered that it was Bobby who'd told him about the camp in the woods. Richard begged his foster mother to let him go with his new best friend. How wrong he'd been. How stupid were they to have been so hopeful about a free camp deep in the woods?

Nothing was free for the dregs of the earth like them.

The unwanted boys.

Richard returned to the coffeeshop where he and Bobby had met up about a year ago, hoping he might turn up. It was a long shot, but Bobby always seemed so comfortable there that Richard figured he was a regular. He approached the cashier.

"Hi there. I was wondering if you knew Bobby Payton?" he asked. "He's a friend of mine and I seem to have lost his number."

"Bobby? Bobby the schoolteacher?" the cashier asked. Richard was surprised to hear that. After all that happened, he didn't think Bobby should ever be around any kids.

"Yeah, that one. You wouldn't by any chance know what school he works at?"

"Sure, it's the one in the Cal Young neighborhood," the cashier said. "I don't know exactly what the school's called, but I think he lives around there. He told me he likes walking to work."

"Oh, cool. Has he been in today?" Richard tried to keep the stress out of his voice.

"Not yet," she said. "He usually comes in about two hours from now. Want a coffee while you sit and wait?"

Richard observed the cashier. She was young, no older than eighteen, and naive to give out so much information on a customer. She'd been lucky she hadn't seen the darkness that some people dwelled in.

"Perfect. I'll take a latte then," Richard said.

"That'll be three twenty-five," she said, and Richard gave her cash.

He grabbed a seat at the window looking out on the street. After his name was called for the latte, he opened an app on his phone and pretended to be reading. He'd told his wife he'd be home late from work even though he'd taken another two weeks of vacation.

His boss hadn't been happy about it, but Richard had six weeks of vacation saved up and his boss couldn't stop him from taking it.

He had to find Bobby.

He had to find out what Bobby was up to.

Richard waited an hour and a half for Bobby to show. He never did. His hands shook from too much caffeine and he'd switched to decaf on his fourth cup. Between his lack of sleep in the last couple of nights and the stress of everything happening, Richard felt he was walking a razor's edge.

He needed to find Bobby. He needed to look into his eyes to know if he was really trying to kill him or if something else had happened that was connected to that camp all those years ago.

He'd seen in the papers that Chris Becker had died.

He'd also been one of the boys at the camp. He had been one of the favorite ones.

Richard remembered how surprised he was when he discovered that Chris had a family. An extremely wealthy family.

The boys later found out Chris Becker's father was an abusive tyrant, and his mother had given up almost everything to get out of the marriage and keep her son away from him. That's how Chris ended up being one of the lost boys.

He checked his watch for the thousandth time. Bobby wasn't coming here today. Today had been almost a wasted day. Luckily, the cashier had given him a piece of information he hadn't known.

Bobby Payton was a teacher. If he could find out which school he worked at, he could track and corner Bobby there. This new angle might work. The plan made Richard feel like some of his control was coming back.

He stared out of the coffee shop window at the Cochran Youth Shelter across the street.

Bobby's smiling face. The fun they had even though they were both terrible at basketball. Rich finally having a friend. The memories sent Richard to his feet.

Those memories were way too painful now. It was time for him to go.

The friendly cashier waved as he walked by. He smiled and waved back.

"Thank you for telling me about Bobby," he said.

"Welcome," she said.

"If you see him again, could you tell him that his friend Richard stopped by? I really need to talk to him," Richard said.

"I'll do that. Have a great day," she said.

Richard stepped out on the street and looked at the

bright blue sky. The cashier was so young. So clean, and sweet, and full of hope.

Richard wished he could have a small piece of that hope, but he knew deep in his heart that all his hope had been left in those dirty bunks during that summer all those years ago.

21

DAY 6 - AFTERNOON

Harri pulled into the driveway of the Daniels Inn and parked.

"We should get you that rental car," she said.

"I was thinking of that. I'll take a ride-share over to the Hertz in town," he said.

"You'll miss having me as your personal driver," Harri said with a smile.

"You bet," Jake said. "What are your next moves on Thomas James?"

"People search," she said. "He mentioned he was a foster care kid. If I can track down some of his old addresses, I might be able to speak to his foster parents. Get a bead on the guy," Harri said.

"You can run those on your computer, right?"

"Yeah, I'll do it here. In my room. I need to find out about this guy. Something about Dan's disappearance really must've spooked him."

She turned off the car and opened her door. The cool

air invigorated her. Harri locked the car behind her and they walked to the entrance of the Inn.

"How serious are they about keeping us away from this?" she asked.

She'd dealt with the FBI before but in a more collaborative capacity.

"It really depends on the agent and how much heat he's getting from upstairs," Jake explained. "It's always about somebody trying to protect their case in this sort of situation. I'm also sure he got crap from Eugene PD asking them to take care of us. PD isn't happy with you and me."

Harri shook her head. It should be about getting results, not about getting the glory. She knew every investigator had to protect their case, but law enforcement across the board should be able to work together.

"If you give me a few minutes, I'll do the search in my room, and then I can drive you back into Eugene for your rental car."

"Good idea," Jake said.

"Give me twenty minutes?"

"I have to go to my room anyway," Jake said.

They parted ways at the top of the stairs. The Inn was quiet. Harri didn't think anyone was staying there besides themselves.

Harri opened the door to her room and knew immediately something was wrong. Shreds of fabric peeked out from below her closet door. Harri pulled her gun out and cleared the room.

Whoever had been in the room was long gone.

She put her latex gloves on before she opened the closet door. All the clothes she'd brought with her had been shredded to ribbons. Dammit! She liked those clothes.

Harri left the room and knocked on Jake's door.

Jake knew something was up from the look on her face.

"What happened?" he asked.

"Somebody's been in my room," Harri finally told him.

"What do you mean?" he asked.

"Someone left Lauren's favorite pin attached to human hair in my bathtub."

"Just now?"

Harri sighed heavily. She would have to tell him everything.

"Can I come in?" she asked.

"Of course," Jake said as he pulled her into his room.

Harri sat on his bed and Jake stood in front of her.

"When I got in last night, I could tell someone had been in my room. That's when I discovered it. It was in the bathtub."

Jake didn't say anything right away, but Harri could tell immediately that he was furious.

"Last night? Why didn't you tell me?"

"I'm not sure. Anyway," Harri said quickly, without answering his question. "Someone came back and shredded all my clothes."

Jake tilted his head, his face showing confusion.

"Shredded?" he asked.

"Come and take a look," she said.

She led him back to her bedroom and gestured to the closet. "Shredded."

"Shredded to ribbons," Jake said. "Do we want to report it?"

"We should report it. I'm clearly being targeted by someone. Were our names in the paper? When Atticus Menlo's body was found?"

"I'm not sure," Jake said as he pulled out his phone and made the phone call. "I'm calling Gavin French."

Harri nodded and swore. She was going to have to get a whole new set of clothes, a massive irritation she did not need right now.

As Jake explained the situation to Gavin, Harri searched on her phone for the nearest mall. It happened to be in the neighborhood nearest the middle school Atticus went to.

"I found a place I can get some new clothes," she said when Jake got off the phone.

"Gavin is sending some uniforms out," Jake said.

"They won't find anything. The last time he left something behind he'd cleaned up all evidence of himself. He's too good."

"Sit down, Harri."

She'd never heard this commanding tone in his voice directed at her. She sat down at the table and he sat across from her.

"I'm beginning to worry about your safety, Harri," Jake said.

"I'm a cop, remember," she said. "I know how to take care of myself. I have a gun."

Jake nodded. "I can't work like this."

Harri knew what he meant.

"I know," she began. "I should have told you last night. It's just that..."

"We have to be honest with each other, Harri. We can't hold out on each other. That's not going to work."

Harri didn't know what to say, so she just nodded.

"We should leave this place. Their security obviously needs help."

"I don't want to leave. This place feels like home,"

Harri replied. "Anyway, it's already been compromised, so what's the point of going somewhere new?"

"Then we don't leave computers or other sensitive materials around."

Harri looked around her room. "We can't let him push us out. We can't show him he's winning or getting to us."

"I hear you, but I'm still concerned," Jake said.

"These are just clothes. They can be replaced."

"But you can't be replaced," Jake said.

He leaned forward and took both her hands in his.

"I will take every precaution," Harri said.

Jake didn't look convinced.

"I'm going to the mall to get new clothes and then off to find Thomas James. Like we spoke about."

He threw up his hands. "What about the police?"

"Can't you deal with them?" Harri asked.

She didn't want to hear anything from Gavin. This was a perfect excuse for them to push her out of town.

"I didn't find something of Lauren's in the bathtub. You should stay here and talk to them first," Jake said.

"This gives them more ammunition," she said.

"Harri, this is madness. Stay and search for Thomas James online. The cops will be here in twenty minutes. They'll take your statement and then we can go get you some new clothes."

Harri shook her head. "I can drop you off at the car rental place. Let's just follow the original plan."

She didn't know why that was so important to her, but it was.

"Yes, ma'am," he said. "You can work on my computer in my room. Your laptop is evidence now. I'll talk to Mack about better security in this place."

Jake left her in his room and Harri launched herself into getting addresses for Thomas James.

Closer to half an hour later, two uniforms Harri didn't recognize took down her and Jake's statements. Harri was relieved that Gavin didn't come to give her a new ration of shit.

After the uniforms cleared her room and took what little evidence there was, Harri and Jake finally left the Inn.

Harri dropped Jake off at the rental car place closest to the mall she was going to. To her surprise, the intruder had even shredded her underwear. That really pissed her off.

Whatever message the intruder was trying to send wasn't working. If he thought she'd be scared off that easy, he was wrong. Instead, she believed more than ever that they were close. Close enough to scare the crap out of whoever was behind this. Behind Dan's disappearance. Behind Lauren's death.

22

DAY 6 - AFTERNOON

Harri was not a shopper.

She hadn't been inside a mall in close to a decade and most of the clothes she owned, she'd ordered online. If the clothes didn't fit, she would send them back. She didn't like big crowds and having to try things on in strange little rooms where people had their fingers over everything grossed her out. But today, she had little choice.

The only store she knew that had decently priced clothes was Macy's. She headed straight there, making a mental list of what she'd need, right down to underwear and socks. She figured she needed five of everything to get through another week. She'd start from the first layers to the outer layers and went in search of the lingerie department.

Harri was so thankful she'd left some of her favorite clothes back home in Los Angeles. None of the clothes she cared about had been damaged. If one of her sister's sweaters had been shredded, she would have been heartbroken.

She filled her arms with everything she needed but couldn't find a single salesperson to check her out. She'd circled around twice and found no one with a nametag.

This was the reason everyone shopped online now, she thought sourly. As she walked by the juniors' section for the second time, a voice called out to her. She looked back and saw a man in his mid-40s with sandy blonde hair, a round face, and brown eyes that appeared kind.

"Were you asking me something?" she asked.

"I haven't been able to find anybody who works here, have you?" he asked.

The guy was reading her mind.

"I was just thinking the same thing. I gotta tell you, there's a reason why I only ever shop online."

"Me too, but I have my nephew coming to visit and I wanted to get him something nice," he said.

He lifted a red cable-knit sweater.

"Do you think a fourteen-year-old boy would like something like this?" he asked.

Harri shrugged her shoulders.

"I honestly have no idea," she said. "I have zero insight into what the kids are wearing these days."

"Neither do I," the man laughed. "Which is why I'm asking you, but I guess this is as good as any."

"Sorry," Harri said.

"Can I ask you one more question?"

"Sure," Harri said as she finally caught sight of a salesperson.

"What do you think of these pants?" he asked.

He held up a pair of khakis with pleats in front."

"Only preppies wear pleats," Harri remarked.

"It's not what all the kids are wearing?" he quipped back.

"Honestly, I doubt it," Harri said.

"Really? Pleats aren't in fashion?" he asked, a grin on his face.

"Not for a few decades," Harri smiled back. "I finally found someone." She pointed to the salesperson.

"Better get her before she disappears," he laughed. "Thanks for your help."

Harri nodded good-bye and headed towards the salesperson while waving.

"Hi, there. Can I check out?"

The woman waved her over to an empty cash register and rang her up. Harri paid for her new clothes and got out of there as quickly as she could, knowing she would never step foot into another mall again for at least another decade.

Harri programmed her phone to the first address she'd found for Thomas James and drove straight there. It was a small purple ranch house with a brown lawn. She saw nothing in the yard to indicate a child lived there. She saw no cars in the drive but hoped someone would be home.

She walked to the front door and knocked. A woman with tight white curls answered the door.

"May I help you?" she asked.

"I hope so. I'm looking for Thomas James. He was a foster kid, and this was a prior address listed for him," Harri said.

"I'm sorry. We only moved here about six weeks ago," the lady said.

"Do you know the name of the previous owners?" Harri asked.

"I don't – but I would think the realtor does. Let me get her number for you," the woman said.

She closed the door on Harri and was only gone a few minutes. The door opened again, and the woman handed Harri a business card with the name Dolores Franz on it.

"I so appreciate this," Harri said.

"I hope you find what you're looking for," the woman said.

Harri nodded. "So do I."

She called Dolores when she got back into the car. The woman didn't pick up. The card listed Dolores Franz's address as well and Harri headed straight for her office.

Harri smoothed her hair down as she entered the realtor's office. She put on her best smile and stepped inside to find a middle-aged woman with bright red hair and lipstick to match sitting at the desk.

"I'm here to speak to Dolores Franz," Harri said.

"That's me. What can I do for you?" she asked.

"I am looking for a family who lived at 279 Stepstone Lane?" Harri asked.

"Oh, honey," Dolores Franz said. "I can't possibly give out that kind of information. It's against company policy. Client privacy, you understand."

"How about if you give them a call and see if they'd be willing to speak with me? I'm looking for information on one of their foster kids," Harri said.

"Well, that family doesn't even live in town anymore," Dolores said.

"You do have a phone number for them then?"

"Of course, I do," she said.

"But you're not going to share it with me, and you are also unwilling to call them?" Harri asked.

"What is this all about? I mean, who are you?" Dolores Franz demanded.

"I'm searching for a missing boy. He's been gone for days now and, as I'm sure you can imagine, his parents are desperate to find him."

"Oh, that's awful," the woman softened. "What does that have to do with this family?"

"Their foster kid is missing, too. He was friends with this boy. I need to find them both, and I have no idea where to look."

"Well, why didn't you say that in the first place?" Dolores scolded. "Let me give her a call right now and see if she'd be willing to talk to you."

"Thank you so very much, Dolores," she said.

Dolores picked up the phone and dialed a number. She let it ring several times and then hung up again.

"I'm sorry, she's not answering. But what I could do is give her a call again and leave a message. What is your number dear, so I can give it to her? If she chooses to call you back?" Dolores asked.

"My number is 213-555-0555," Harri said.

Dolores wrote it down. "And your name?"

Harri gave the woman her name but didn't say she was with LAPD.

"Is that all?" she asked.

Harri nodded. This was as far as she would get with this woman.

"Thank you so much," Harri said and left.

She hurried down the walk, stomach in knots. Thomas James was a cipher. Frustrated, she threw her bag into the passenger seat and sat down. She'd try Alan Prentiss's parents next. They had to be home by now.

23

DAY 6 - AFTERNOON

Harri parked her car in front of the Prentiss home and was happy to see both a BMW and a Lexus in the driveway. They had to be home. The Prentiss place was a stately two-story colonial with pretty green clapboard shutters on each window. The entire property looked straight out of a storybook.

Because she knew their son was an addict, had been living on the streets, and was now likely missing, possibly the prey of a pedophile ring, looking at the cheerful home made Harri's heart skip a beat. She walked up to the door and knocked. A blond-haired woman in her 50s appeared in the doorway. She frowned when she saw Harri.

"May I help you?" she asked.

"I'm here about your son Alan Prentiss," Harri said.

The mother's shoulders tensed.

"Have you found his body?" she asked.

"Mrs. Prentiss may I come inside and speak with you?" Harri asked.

"And who are you?" she asked.

"I'm a family friend of Tim Ledeyen. I'm not sure if you've heard, but his son Dan Ledeyen has gone missing. I'm a detective from Los Angeles helping to find him. Tim gave me Alan's name as one of Dan's closest friends," she said.

The woman's mouth formed a thin line. She didn't say a word. Mrs. Prentiss stepped out of the doorway and gestured for Harri to come inside.

"Not sure how I can help. Dan and Alan haven't been friends for a while and we have no contact with Alan," she said.

Harri bit her lip at that. She'd worried that might be the case and wasn't sure if she should share with his parents that Alan might have gone missing, as well.

"Any information you can provide could help me in my search. I'm not sure if I should tell you this, but I've had a difficult time tracking Alan down."

Mrs. Prentiss guided her to a living room awash in pastels. The sofas were upholstered in silk and the pale pink-flowered wallpaper shimmered in the late afternoon sun. The feminine room was incredibly formal.

"Alan can usually be found around the Cochran Youth Shelter downtown. He's been living on the streets for the last year." Mrs. Prentiss spoke stiffly with the demeanor of a defeated, but stoic woman.

"That's where I've looked for him. None of his friends have seen him, either."

"So, you think that Alan and Dan might be together?" Mrs. Prentiss asked.

"Yes."

"If that's the case, then I'm very sorry for Tim and Molly," Mrs. Prentiss said. "Molly told me Dan was out of rehab and it was sticking this time. If he's hanging out with my son, he's using again."

"Do you remember the last time you saw Dan or your son?" Harri asked.

"I haven't seen Dan in at least six months. Alan came around here about three weeks ago. He promised he was clean, but of course, after being here for a night, cash was missing from my wallet again."

Tears formed in the corners of her eyes. "I never learn, but he is, after all, my son," she said.

"Do you have any idea where Alan was staying prior to coming to see you?" Harri asked.

"On the streets around that shelter," Ms. Prentiss said. "When his father first kicked him out of the house, I took to driving the downtown area at night looking for him. Trying to make sure he'd be okay."

"And did you find him down there?" Harri asked.

"Yes. Several times."

Harri wasn't sure how Mrs. Prentiss would take the next question. There was no easy way to ask it. She plunged in.

"How did your son get money for drugs?" Harry asked in a soft voice.

"He and Dan were breaking into cars," Mrs. Prentiss sighed and dabbed her eyes with the back of her hand. "From what Alan told me they were bringing in enough to support their habits. Then after Dan went into rehab this last time, Alan couldn't keep it going. It seemed to me that Alan was lost without Dan. I can only imagine what he had to do for money. But he refused to get help, so my husband refused to allow him to come home," she said.

Mrs. Prentiss' expression was one of weariness. The pain of having a son with such a demon on his back was hard to witness. A cellphone rang from somewhere inside a bag. Mrs. Prentiss reached for her purse.

"Excuse me, I've been waiting for my husband to call," she explained as she rummaged through her bag for the ringing phone. When she pulled it out, she frowned.

"My God, it's the police," she said as she answered the call.

Harri watched as the woman listened to the caller on the other line.

Mrs. Prentiss paled, and she sank deeper into the sofa with her hand over her mouth. The look of shock was so complete that Harri knew something terrible had happened to Alan. Mrs. Prentiss hung up the phone and focused back on Harri, her eyes wide and uncomprehending.

"They found Alan?" Harri asked.

"About four hours ago. They said they're sending someone out and wanted to warn me about the media. They said whatever I do, don't talk to the media."

Harri's heart sank. If the police were on their way, she'd better leave.

"Alan was found in the woods. Like that poor Atticus boy."

Harri fought the urge to get up and run out of the house. The cases were converging, as she knew they would. She had to leave before the cops arrived.

"What can I do for you, Mrs. Prentiss?" Harri asked.

Her stomach twisted in pain, but she had to do what she could for this poor woman who'd just heard that her son had been murdered and his body dumped in the woods.

Her heart thumped as she waited for the woman to respond.

"I have to call my husband. I have to call my husband and tell him," she said.

"I'll stay with you until he gets here," Harri said.

Mrs. Prentiss was so pale Harri worried the woman might pass out.

"That won't be necessary," Mrs. Prentiss said as she pulled herself straight.

She gained back some composure and, by her demeanor, Harri knew she wanted her to leave.

"I'm so very sorry for your loss," Harri said, relieved that she could go.

She stood up and looked at the woman awkwardly. "I'll let myself out. I'm so deeply sorry for your loss," she said again.

Harri found herself tongue-tied as she witnessed the woman's grief. Various emotions passed on her face. Mrs. Prentiss opened her mouth and closed it again. The woman finally found her voice as she stood up.

"We lost Alan years ago," she said. "I've been waiting for this phone call since the last rehab was such an utter failure. Good luck finding Dan. I hope he's out there alive somewhere. Bring him home."

Harri nodded and left the woman standing in the middle of her formal living room. As she let herself out and hurried back to her car it occurred to her that Mrs. Prentiss kept her house so beautifully because the rest of her life was such an ugly mess.

She drove away in a panic. Where was Dan Ledeyen? Was he being held somewhere, or would he be the next boy found washed clean in the woods?

She called Jake. He picked up immediately.

"Jake," she croaked.

"Harri? My god, what is it?"

"They found Alan Prentiss in the woods like Atticus Menlo. I was with his mother when the police called her," she said in a rush.

Jake exhaled on the other end of the line.

"I was worried about that," he said. "Where are you now? Let's meet up."

"No, I'm okay," Harri said. "I'm okay. I have to talk to Tim again. I feel like we still haven't accounted for all of Dan's movements in the forty-eight hours before his abduction."

"The deaths are out of order," Jake said. "Dan's body should have been found next. He was the second boy abducted. Alan was the third. Something's wrong here. I don't know if the profile is off or could something have happened to bump Alan in front of Dan," Jake said.

"I wondered the same thing. But we can leave that to the police even if Dan was taken by the same perpetrator."

"Right," Jake said.

"Have you met with Dr. Brand yet?"

"Not yet. I'm driving up now. Are you going to tell him?"

Harri hadn't considered telling Tim. It wouldn't be good for him to find out on the news, though.

"I'll let him know when I see him. Another devastated family," Harri said. "I hope Dr. Brand has pinpointed the location of at least one of the camps."

"I'll call you after," Jake said and hung up.

Harri fought back the nausea as butterflies invaded her stomach. She drove to the Ledeyen home gripping the wheel so hard her knuckles turned white. She'd have to watch another parent's face as they processed their deepest fear about their child. Harri desperately wished she had better news to tell him.

Something told her Dan was almost out of time.

24

DAY 6 - AFTERNOON

The Ledeyen house was only several blocks over from the Prentiss home, but the neighborhood looked much different. The lawns were not as manicured, and the homes were modest. It didn't matter whether these families were rich or poor or which neighborhood they lived in. The devastation of addiction was all-encompassing. This fracture in each of these families gave predators a healthy number of victims and a hunting ground that grew each day. This pain was such a waste, Harri thought.

She parked the car in front of the house and scrolled through the breaking news on her phone. The discovery of Alan's body made national headlines as Atticus Menlo's had. If the killer wanted this kind of attention, he was definitely getting it. Harri turned off her phone and chewed on her lip. They had to know about Alan already. His death was already all over the news.

She heaved open the door and stepped out. Exhaustion washed over her as she made her way to the front door. Molly had it open before Harri reached the top step.

"We've just heard," she said.

Harri shook her head, unsure of what to say next. She was relieved she wasn't the one to break the news.

"Alan's mother called you?" she asked.

Molly nodded and Tim appeared behind her.

"She didn't tell us how it happened," Molly said. "She just told us that Alan was dead."

Harri let out a deep breath and followed them into the house.

Damn.

"You're going to hear it on the news, so I might as well tell you. Alan was found in the same way Atticus Menlo was," she said.

Tim led them back to the kitchen.

Harri had been to this house so often before the change in the atmosphere struck her hard. There was no warmth here. A faint smell of rotten food permeated the air. The stack of dirty dishes in the sink looked about to topple over.

"I put the coffee on," Tim said as he smoothed his unbrushed hair back with his hand. "Would you like some?"

"I'd prefer water if that's okay," Harri said, worried the extra caffeine hit would send her nerves over the edge.

Tim opened one of the cupboards and chose a glass. He filled it with water from the sink and handed it to her.

"Thank you," she said.

Molly sat down on one side of her and Tim on the other. They both leaned in and Harri felt trapped. She hated that she had no new information for them.

"How did you find out about Alan? Did the police call you?" Tim asked.

Harri sipped her water before answering.

"The police warned me off that case. I was with Mrs. Prentiss, asking her about Alan and Dan's relationship when she got the phone call," she explained.

"Does this killer have our boy?" Molly asked, her eyes wide and her pupils dilated. The woman was terrified.

"We don't know that for certain," Harri tried to reassure her. "The timeline isn't entirely matching up. Alan disappeared after Dan, but his body was just found. This is a good thing for us since it indicates two possible scenarios. Either this individual doesn't have Dan or he's keeping Dan alive for some reason. Either scenario makes me think that Dan is still alive."

Molly covered her mouth with her hands to muffle her cry.

Harri fidgeted in her seat.

"I'm doing everything I can to find Dan. That is my only objective right now and it's the reason I came here today," she said.

"Anything you need," Tim said.

He looked as if he'd aged ten years since she'd seen him two days ago. His clothes hung from his body and he had the sunken eyes of a man who hadn't had a decent night's sleep in weeks.

Molly's face was puffy and red and reminded Harri of her own mother in those first weeks after Lauren's disappearance. She prayed that Molly stayed strong. Harri's mother had cracked and killed herself within that first year.

"I haven't been able to map out exactly what Dan was doing the day before he disappeared," Harri said.

"I've retraced his steps on the day of his abduction. I've spoken with the Starbucks manager and with witnesses who saw him enter and leave the job interview. His schedule on that day doesn't provide us with much to go on since he was home before he left for the job interview." Harri paused. "Where did Dan go the day before?"

"The day before was similar," Molly choked out. "He'd become a real homebody after rehab. He'd lost all his friends from before he got into the drugs. He was staying away from the people who were still using. I enjoyed his company. I had my son back."

Harri waited as the woman gathered herself together again.

"He was home until he left for his GRE class at Eugene Community College. His class runs for three hours," Molly added.

"He came home directly after," Tim cut in.

"And what time is this GRE class?" Harri asked.

"It's from three-thirty to six-thirty. The class meets today, too. In an hour," Molly said checking the clock hanging over the door leading to the patio outside.

"Do you know the instructor's name?"

Molly shook her head.

"I don't know it either," Tim offered.

"It's the only GRE prep class at that time," Molly continued. "Dan had a hard time finding a class in the late afternoon. He told us he'd been lucky he got into that one."

"Could I see a schedule of his to find the classroom I should stakeout?" Harri said in a light tone.

Neither Molly nor Tim caught the reference.

"I'll go there today and talk to his classmates. Maybe they can give me more names of people I can interview."

"Are you thinking that whoever took Dan knew him? This wasn't a random grab?' Tim asked, stumbling on the words.

"If Dan had been shoved into a car, I think more people would have witnessed that since it's rare," Harri said. "I think Dan knew the person who pulled up to him and he got into their car willingly. That's why the witnesses are so vague on details. The action was too commonplace."

Her explanation was the most plausible one, she thought.

Dan could have met his kidnapper in class and not in fact at Starbucks the next day. Had he seen someone he was friendly with; it would be that much easier for him to get into a car with the individual.

"You mentioned he was staying away from all his friends," Harri continued. "Did he do anything else outside of the GRE class and the NA meetings down at the Cochran Youth Shelter?" she asked.

"He was sticking close to home," Molly said. "Reading a lot of books and keeping himself away from people. It was the only way he said he could stay away from temptation."

Tears streamed down her face and she wiped them away. Harri saw anger brimming below the surface of her grief.

"Let me find that schedule for you," Tim said and left the kitchen.

Harri took Molly's hand in her own. "I won't stop looking until I bring him home," she said. "He's out there somewhere. Alive."

Harri didn't know why she added that, but she believed it, fervently even.

Molly nodded and wiped her nose with a tissue. The

familiar gesture reminded Harri of her mom. She'd taken her mom's hand in hers and promised her that she'd bring Lauren home somehow. She'd been fifteen years old at the time, a child attempting to comfort her mother. The look on her mother's face back then mirrored Molly's now.

Neither woman believed her, however much they wanted to.

Harri let go of Molly's hand when she heard Tim's footsteps outside of the kitchen. Without finding Dan, her words could never take the pain of unknowing away from them. Harri knew that all too well.

Tim came back with a single sheet of paper. "The class is held in Mills Hall. It's Room 205. I think Dan mentioned it was a large auditorium on the first floor."

Tim handed the schedule to Harri. She snapped a photo of it with her phone and placed it on the kitchen table.

"Take care of each other and get some sleep."

Molly stared blankly back at her.

"I know that sounds cliché, but sleep will help with the pain. And you need to keep strong. For Dan's sake when he finally gets home."

Tim nodded but Molly was gone. Most likely inhabiting her own personal hell. Harri gulped down the water and stood up.

"If I'm going to make it to this class, I have to leave. I'll see myself out."

Tim nodded but didn't stand up. Molly stared out the window to the woods beyond as if Harri had said nothing. Harri couldn't imagine the thoughts running through her head.

She walked out of the kitchen and out the front door. The moment she got outside, she inhaled deeply. She hadn't realized she'd been holding her breath until that very moment.

The pain of this was so familiar. Her chest constricted and Harri pressed her hand hard against where her heart was. She knew this pain. She lived it every day.

25

DAY 6 – AFTERNOON

Harri Harper stood outside classroom 205 in Mills Hall watching the students file in. She had made it with ten minutes to spare before class. She parked herself to the right of the door, a photo of Dan Ledeyen in hand. She flashed it at every student who walked by, asking if they knew him. Most students shook their heads no and declined to speak with her. Two giggling teenagers strolled by her, one of them glancing back. Harri used that as her opening.

"Hi, do you guys have a second before class?" she asked.

The blonde-haired girl rolled her eyes and looked at her friend. "We're not really interested in whatever you're selling," she said in a snooty voice.

"I'm here about Dan Ledeyen," Harri said and held up the photo. "He's in your class."

"I've never seen him before," the snooty blonde said.

The quiet one nodded.

"I've seen him in class," she said in a small shy voice.

"He's gone missing. I'm helping the family locate him," Harri said.

The shy girl's eyes widened. "Missing? Like did he run away or something?" she asked.

Harri judged her age to be close to seventeen and wondered why she was taking GED classes at the local community college and not attending an actual high school.

"His parents have no idea where he is," Harri said. "Did you see him the last time he was in class? That would've been this last Tuesday."

"Oh, I remember him. He walked in late and the teacher kind of gave him shit for it," the snooty girl said.

How surprising that suddenly she knew exactly who he was. She seemed to Harri to be one of those girls that always needed to be at the center of attention.

"I thought you said you never saw him before," Harri said.

She didn't want to embarrass the girl, but at the same time calling the snooty girl out on her crap might give Harri points with the shy girl. By the look on the shy girl's face, Harri was correct.

"Did either of you see him after class?" she asked.

"I did," Shy Girl said. "He was arguing with our teacher when we were all getting ready to leave."

"And are you sure it was an argument?" Harri asked, ears perking up.

"I was pretty close to the front, where they were. I was waiting to ask my own question and I noticed our teacher was getting really upset," the shy girl said.

"What's your teacher's name?" Harri asked.

The paperwork Tim had found didn't list the teacher's name on it.

"His name is Professor Robert Payton," the snooty girl said.

"How do you know he was getting upset?" she asked the shy girl.

"It was his face. He turned all red and flushed and he was making his hands into fists," the shy girl said.

"That's a peculiar detail to remember," Harri commented. "What made you notice that?"

"My boyfriend has anger issues," the shy girl said.

Her voice became flat and emotionless when she said that. Harri read between those lines.

"And did you see Dan leave?" she asked.

"No. I gave up on waiting to ask my question and decided to ask him the next class," the shy girl said.

"Is your professor in class already?" Harri asked.

"I don't think so. He's also a high school teacher at Milbourne. He sometimes gets here a little bit late because of traffic," the snooty girl said.

Harri's ears pricked up.

Robert Payton was a teacher at the same school that Atticus had gone to. And it was the same school that Chris Becker had been seen staking out. That couldn't be a coincidence.

"Is he in the room now?" Harri asked and peeked around the door into the large auditorium.

The shy girl did the same and scanned the room.

"Is that him?" Harri asked, pointing to the older man sitting behind the desk.

"No. That's Professor Tremaine. He's here sometimes when Professor Payton is running late," the snooty girl said.

"He's generally like ten minutes late for every class," the shy girl said.

"Have either of you had any difficult interactions with Professor Payton? Do you like him?"

The snooty girl rolled her eyes again. "I mean he's okay. Kind of boring."

The shy girl said nothing. Harri figured she was the one that really paid attention to people's emotions and temperaments anyway. If the shy girl had a boyfriend with anger management problems, then she was pretty used to checking in on him constantly to see what temperature he was for her own safety."

"He has strange moods," the shy girl said.

"What kind of moods?" Harri asked.

"He gets super angry about things being out of order. It's more than most normal teachers do. It bothers him a lot when he feels that anyone's misbehaving in class," the shy girl explained.

"This GED class is college age or high school age students?" Harri asked.

"I think most of the students are our age," the snooty girl said.

"And what are your ages?" Harri asked.

"I am seventeen," the snooty girl said.

"Sixteen," the shy girl said.

"How come you guys aren't going to a normal high school?" Harri asked.

Snooty girl folded her arms across her chest in a defensive pose. "I got expelled," she said.

"I did, too," the shy girl said.

"Really? Did you two get expelled together?" Harri asked.

She wondered if the snooty girl had been the ring-leader and the shy girl followed her lead.

"We came from the same school. We got in trouble at

the same time," the snooty girl said confirming Harri's suspicions.

"Thank you, girls, so very much for your time."

"I hope you find him," the shy girl said. "He seemed nice."

"Did you ever speak to him?" Harri asked.

The shy girl shook her head no.

Harri guessed that might have been the case.

"Thanks again," Harri said.

She had a name and another connection to Milbourne High School. Dan had fought with this man the day before he disappeared. The teacher showed an authoritarian streak to his students and had a temper. That combination spelled trouble.

Harri attempted to speak to several more students, but the class was beginning, and everyone rushed by her to get to their seats. Harri had the information she wanted anyway. She didn't think anyone else would speak to her.

She walked down the hall with her fingers tingling. They sometimes did that when her adrenaline overflowed her system. After taking in the pain of Dan's father and Alan's mother, she wanted concrete, actionable steps to find Dan. Those girls had given her that.

Harri decided to snoop around Milbourne High School to see what other dirt she could collect on Robert Payton. She pulled out her phone to call Jake but stopped herself. The lead was a good one, albeit still a little flimsy.

Harri clutched her phone as she left Mills Hall. She'd call Jake after visiting Milbourne. He might take issue with her going there because of the Atticus case. They'd agreed to keep out of that case. Even if Harri was following a Dan lead, that wouldn't matter much to

Eugene PD. Better to fly under the radar until she had something more concrete.

It did make her wonder why the school kept coming up in the investigation. It couldn't be the only high school in the area, yet there had to be another connection. She walked faster as the wind whipped through her hair. The wind had a bite to it, and she relished its freshness. So much nicer than Los Angeles, she thought as she got back into her car.

Milbourne High looked like a traditional school out of a movie. It had a red-brick exterior with decorative carved windows on all three floors. It looked like a building from the 1930s. School was already long out, and the sports teams must have finished up because the visitor's parking lot was relatively empty. Harri hoped she'd be able to catch someone there to talk to. Even a janitor. She parked nearest the entrance and was happily surprised to find the front door still open.

Harri followed the signs to the principal's office and smiled when she saw the woman inside. She pushed the door open, her smile widening.

"Hi, I'm looking for Robert Payton. He's a teacher here," Harri asked the young plus-sized woman wearing a Hawaiian graphic wrap-around dress who was sitting at the front desk.

"What do you need with Bobby?" the secretary asked.

"What's your name?" Harri asked.

"What's yours?" the secretary shot back.

Harri smiled again to help with the tension in the room. She leaned over conspiratorially.

"I'm trying to serve him papers," Harri lied. "School looks like it's out. Have I missed him?"

"School ended about an hour ago," the secretary said softening up a tinge.

"I went to his class at Eugene Community College, but he wasn't there, either."

"Have you tried his house?"

"That information wasn't on file. You wouldn't by any chance have it?" Harri asked sweetly. "I've been tracking him all afternoon and I just want to deliver these papers."

She hoped that Robert "Bobby" Payton had rubbed the secretary the wrong way and maybe she would divulge some information she shouldn't.

The secretary scrunched up her nose as if she was smelling something bad. So, Bobby Payton wasn't the most beloved of characters.

"What did he do this time?" the secretary asked in a low voice.

"I can't really say, but it's not good," Harri said. "Do you know if he lives somewhere around here?"

"He must. He walks to school every day. Don't ask me for his address again, though. I can't give it to you."

"I understand," Harri said. "Would you by any chance be willing to tell me if he was at school this past Wednesday?" she asked.

Might as well see if he had an alibi for the day of Dan's disappearance.

"Can't really tell you that, either," the secretary said.

"How about this. Did you see him that day?" Harri asked.

"That was three days ago?" the secretary wondered.

Harri nodded.

"I don't really recall seeing him, but that doesn't mean anything. If he didn't come in the office for anything, then I wouldn't have seen him. I have my lunch break, of course, but it's at a different time than the teachers."

Harri nodded and thanked the woman.

She'd inadvertently slipped and told her Robert Payton lived in the neighborhood. That should be enough to run another person's search for his address. Harri headed for her car to get some privacy. Once inside, she would start her search for his address. She was in the neighborhood. She should definitely pay him a visit.

26

DAY 6 - AFTERNOON

Harri's pulse raced as she hurried to the rental car parked in the visitor's lot. Her excitement fought a growing apprehension as she zeroed in on Robert Payton as the man who'd kidnapped Dan. He was the first real lead she'd come across in Dan's disappearance. There were too many coincidences in the timeline for him not to be a suspect. Judging from the way both the students and the secretary spoke of him, he was a complex man who inspired fear in people.

And he'd likely done suspect things before.

But if she was mistaken, she'd be wasting precious time in zeroing on the wrong man as the time ticked away for Dan. Something in her gut told her he didn't have much time left. The short time span between when Alan Prentiss was taken and when he turned up dead was alarming. She had no access to the particulars in the case, but she wondered if there were differences in the way that Atticus and Alan had died.

She knew that Dan had to have been taken by the same man who killed Atticus and probably Alan. Obviously, she couldn't prove it yet, but all her years on the force stood behind her gut feeling.

First though, was to find Robert Payton's address.

She opened the car door and sat in the driver's seat. She pulled up the people search website she'd been using while she was in Eugene and typed in his name and the zip code of the school. She filled out her credit card details and hit send.

Harri waited for the site to process her card and pull up his information.

The amount of information you could discover on people for a fee was shocking and she'd promised herself that she'd scrub the internet of her info as soon as she got back to Los Angeles. But for now, she was thankful for the help since she didn't have the contacts up here to help her find the people she needed. Not while the Eugene PD and the local FBI office wanted her gone. The insistence from both agencies for her and Jake to leave town still bothered her, but she didn't have time to delve deeper into that.

Dan was still out there, and they were running out of time.

Nausea coiled through her body as she remembered the sight of Atticus Menlo lying in the woods. Dan would not end up that way.

The information on Robert Payton finally came up and Harri mapped the address. It was only two blocks away. She could leave the car and walk there.

Harri scrunched up her nose. Would that be a good idea, though? What if she needed a fast getaway?

If she drove there, she could lose the element of surprise. It's harder to see someone coming up the walk quietly versus a car pulling up and parking on the street. Also, the neighbors. She didn't want to telegraph her presence there, especially if she was wrong. She would walk.

Harri grabbed her purse and got out of the car. She clicked the locks closed and checked her phone for the map. The directions led her across the parking lot and to the left. She clicked the car doors locked one last time and headed for Robert Payton's house.

She'd arrived on his street when a message from Jake made her phone buzz.

Jake: They leaked Alan's crime scene photo to the press.

Harri stopped walking.

Oh, his poor parents, she thought.

She typed back.

Harri: You have a link?

Jake: Here it is.

A link to a local news website popped up.

Harri clicked on it.

Shivers ran up and down her body and she stumbled over a piece of broken sidewalk.

The red cable-knit sweater.

The khaki pants with the pleats in front.

The exact outfit the man in the mall asked her opinion on.

• • •

Every hair on Harri's skin stood on end. She stood frozen as shivers ran up and down her spine. She choked on her spit and gasped out a breath.

He was following her.

The man who'd killed those boys had been in her room. He'd dared to talk to her, and she hadn't noticed.

That was the worst part of it. Before the first intrusion into her room, Harri had no idea she was being watched.

Harri forced her head to move.

She scanned her surroundings. The bright sunny afternoon hadn't brought the citizens of this neighborhood out. There was no one on the street as far as she could see. Most likely they were still at work.

She placed her hand on the holster of her gun. She unclipped the strap that held the gun in place but didn't pull it out. Yet.

Harri let out a deep breath and turned towards the direction she'd just come from. The safety of her car called to her, but her brain kept stuttering on the same thought.

She stopped walking and frowned.

The timing didn't fit.

Alan had already been found by the time she'd seen the man in the mall. So, the man couldn't have dressed him in the clothes he'd shown her. But he wanted to show off that he knew what Alan Prentiss was wearing anyway.

To let her know that he'd been right under her nose and she hadn't known it was him.

Why else would he have shown her the outfit a dead boy wore?

Or was this just a bizarre coincidence?

No, Harri thought. The outfit was too weird for it to be just a coincidence. Harri recalled the man's features as nondescript but pleasant. A perfect mask to hide behind.

She speed-dialed Jake.

He didn't answer.

"Jake," Harri said. "The outfit that Alan Prentiss was wearing. A man came up to me at the mall asking about an outfit for his nephew. He showed me that exact red cable-knit sweater and the front-pleated khaki pants. He was in his 50s. Medium build. Round face. Brown eyes, blonde hair. Around six foot two maybe. I didn't hear an accent..."

Before she could finish, his voicemail cut her off with a message his mailbox was full. Harri hung up and tried dialing again. This time the phone was busy.

Damn, she thought.

She checked the map she'd been following, the blue dot flashing at her. Robert Payton's house was right there. If he was the man in the mall, she'd recognize him immediately.

She opened her contacts and found Detective Gavin French's number. Her finger hovered over the button. This was his case. He'd want her to call him. If she was in his shoes, she'd want the call. But they'd told her to stay away from the case. They'd called her lieutenant to discredit her. To force her home.

She needed more evidence than a hunch and a coincidence. Instead of dialing the number, she typed in Robert Payton and clicked on the images tab. She scanned the men's faces that came up with the search. None of them was the man from the mall. That didn't mean much. Maybe he didn't have an online presence.

Her heart thumped in her chest.

She had no backup.

Jake didn't know where she was.

She texted him the address to Robert Payton's house as well as his name. Just in case.

Feeling better about her decision to keep Jake appraised of her location, she crossed the street and sauntered up Robert Payton's walk.

27

DAY 6 - AFTERNOON

Jake Tepesky checked the time. He was fifteen minutes late for his meeting with Dr. Jasmine Brand. He sped up and hoped she'd still be there.

First, there had been a long line at the rental car office. Then, when he finally sat in the car, he'd been so concerned over Harri's not telling him immediately about the hair and ornament she'd found in her bathtub, he'd lost his way on the drive over to the coffeeshop. And, of course, now he couldn't find a place to park. He'd driven around the block twice before finally finding a metered spot. He pulled in, his mind still on Harri.

She was a decorated cop and could take care of herself, as she so readily reminded him. At the same time, this was the most personal of cases and there was a reason law enforcement frowned on cops investigating cases involving family members. He found he'd done his best work when he had distance, however small, on a case. Harri had no distance.

If he was honest with himself, he didn't have much distance, either. Lauren had been his best friend. He'd loved her like a sister. She was his family. That was a problem, too. He was too close, just like Harri.

Jake didn't feel good about where the direction of their investigation was going. The deeper they delved, the murkier this case became. He didn't like the feeling of being so lost and in the dark, cut off from resources, out on their own. It didn't bode well for them.

He and Harri had reconnected only recently, but he felt as if they'd never lost contact. And what he knew of her made him more concerned about how far she would go to discover what happened to Lauren. He'd done something similar when he first joined the FBI. Every case was THE case. It hadn't worked out well for him.

These thoughts followed him all the way into the coffeeshop. Dr. Jasmine Brand stood up when she saw him and waved.

"Where's Detective Harper? I thought she'd be joining us?" she asked.

Dr. Brand gestured to the empty seat next to her and Jake sat down. Dr. Brand seemed nervous, he thought. She kept picking at her jeans and fiddling with her hair. Jake didn't think her nervousness had anything to do with him. He knew she wouldn't like what he was about to tell her.

"Is everything all right, Dr. Brand?" he asked.

"Yes," she said too quickly. "Yeah, of course. Why?"

"If you don't mind my saying so, you seem nervous."

Dr. Brand straightened and her hands stilled. "I'm not."

Jake nodded. She wasn't going to like what he was about to say.

"I want to be honest with you," he began.

"Eugene PD doesn't want you around here anymore?" she asked.

"How did you know?" Jake asked with a laugh.

"It wasn't hard to see that at the crime scene. When we found that boy..."

"How are you doing after that? It's hard to come across a body, even more when the victim is so young."

Her fingers fidgeted again. "I've seen bones that young before," she stated flatly.

"I'm sorry to hear that."

"Me, too."

"Going back to all the people that don't want me and Detective Harper helping here. This includes the local FBI office who warned us off, too," Jake said with a grimace.

"Why the FBI?" Dr. Brand asked as she sipped her coffee.

Jake checked the people sitting around them. A couple was at a far table and a guy with a laptop sat two tables over. Beyond that, the cafe was empty. He leaned in anyway, to make sure he wasn't heard.

"You didn't hear this from me," he said.

Dr. Brand nodded.

"The man who was found shot, the one with the photo of that camp and Detective Harper's sister?"

"Yes," she prompted.

"Certain images were uncovered on his computer. These images prompted his case to be taken over by the FBI. They warned us off, too," he said.

"Okay," Dr. Brand nodded. "Okay, I've done a lot of research about the camps that were granted permission to use federal land. Will this research be directly connected to the case that was taken over by the FBI?"

"We don't know. We have no idea if the photo has anything to do with what the FBI found on Chris Becker's computer. We aren't concerned about the Becker case as it stands. We're trying to uncover the exact location of the camp."

"I see," Dr. Brand said.

She shifted uncomfortably in her seat.

"We don't want to drag you into anything that makes you uncomfortable. If you want to share the information you've uncovered with us, we can go to the locations on our own," he said.

"You won't know where you'd be going," she said. "This specific camp I'm looking at is difficult to get to. It's unique since the site is on an island in the middle of the forest. There's only one path I could find going to the lake which is kind of odd. It's a ride out to the mouth of the trail. The lake isn't huge, but we'll need a boat to get out there."

"I don't want any trouble coming your way," Jake said.

"You said this camp doesn't have anything to do with the present case?"

"I haven't found a connection yet, but that doesn't mean there isn't one." He wanted to be as honest with her as he possibly could.

"So, there is a possibility of there being a connection then?"

"Anything is possible at this point," Jake admitted.

Dr. Brand sighed. After several moments she spoke again.

"The Willamette State Park is federal land. We have every right to go searching in it. It's in a different part of the park than where the first boy was found."

"I wanted to be as forthright with you as possible. Whatever may have happened back at this camp has consequences now."

"Is the camp connected with the Atticus Menlo case? Or the other boy they found today?" Dr. Brand asked.

"I don't know how it connects to the Atticus Menlo case or the Chris Becker case, or even Alan Prentiss. Lauren Harper being photographed with those boys is a crime since she was abducted. We haven't been able to identify any of the boys yet. There could be several cases connected to that photograph."

"Which case was Eugene PD warning you off of?" she asked.

"They wanted us to stay away from the Menlo and Prentiss murders," Jake said.

"And the FBI is Chris Becker?" she asked.

Jake nodded. "Tell me about this camp."

"It was hard to track down. Someone on the state level sealed the records about fifteen years ago. I was lucky to have found mention of it in a newspaper from the early 90s and when I went looking for it on a map, I found the name of it. You know what the really weird thing is?"

"What?" Jake asked.

"The site of the camp, in fact, the island itself had been scrubbed from any maps after the year 2000."

"That sounds deliberate. How was the camp created?"

"The federal government sold a lease to a very wealthy man named Jerome Wexler. Construction of the camp started in June of 1991. The facilities were open the next summer. The newspaper article stated it was a year-round camp for troubled boys," Dr. Brand handed him a clipped article.

"This is the only article it was mentioned in?" Jake asked.

"That's correct. They named it Camp Nightwood."

"Who was Jerome Wexler?" Jake asked. "Did the article mention anything about him?"

"He was a wealthy finance guy. Something to do with real estate. He apparently had political aspirations in the 90s. He ran for governor in 1995, but I couldn't find any other mention of him after that initial run."

"He lost, I assume," Jake asked.

"Yes. Some scandal waylaid his campaign and he dropped out of the race. He fled the country, and I found no mention of him again in Oregon," Dr. Brand said. "That kind of research is not my area of expertise. I did find land records of the deal for the island. It was called Black Rock Island."

"Who owns it now?" Jake asked.

"It's federal land again. The lease expired."

She opened a map and showed him the general vicinity of the lake and island. To Jake, it looked small in a vast area of forest.

"When can I get out there? If I grabbed Harri, could we make it tonight?"

"If we went today, we'd have to go in the next hour and a half. We only have about four hours of daylight left. It's about a half-hour hike to the lake and it would take about an hour to get there." She looked outside again and checked her watch. "Maybe it would be best if we waited until tomorrow. Hiking out there in the dark wouldn't be the easiest. It's not a well-known trail and searching for anything in the dark is tricky."

"If you could lead us to the start of the trail, I think Harri will want to take that chance. Dan Ledeyen is still missing, and I have a feeling he might be out there," Jake said.

This surprised Dr. Brand.

"I thought you said you weren't investigating the boys?" Dr. Brand asked.

"I'm not. Not officially. We have to bring Dan Ledeyen home, though."

"Why do you think he's out there?"

"A hunch. This camp is the start of whatever is going on here."

"You have the maps," Dr. Brand hesitated. "I'm not sure if I can join this expedition. I hope you understand."

"I totally understand that," Jake said, and he did. "Do you mind showing me again on the map exactly where we're going?"

Dr. Brand nodded and showed him the start of the trail and where it would lead them to the island.

He checked his phone and swiped to open it. It was frozen. He pressed the two buttons to restart it as he gathered up the map.

"Thank you so much for the help. We both really appreciate it."

Dr. Brand nodded. "I hope you don't mind my asking, but could you please not mention where you got this map from?"

"Absolutely. I'll keep your involvement out of it. Thank you."

Dr. Brand finished her coffee and grabbed her purse. She stood up and Jake followed her out the door. They said their good-byes and Jake walked back to his car, constantly checking his phone. It was still booting up.

Jake got into the car and waited for his phone to go back online. He sat there for another couple of minutes, his heart pounding. When the phone finally refreshed, Jake typed in his passcode and messages from Harri popped up.

She'd gone to a man's house. His name was Robert

Payton and she'd included his address. Jake hadn't heard the name before. He saw he had a voicemail also waiting from her.

He called her first. Harri's phone went straight to voicemail. That wasn't like her. He listened to the message and gripped the phone as he listened to her story about the man in the mall. He shouldn't have left her alone. Dammit.

Jake slammed the wheel several times. Something happened to Harri. He knew it.

He dialed Detective Gavin French as he peeled out of the parking spot towards Robert Payton's house. Gavin picked up on the first ring.

"Harri's in trouble."

28

DAY 6 - AFTERNOON

Harri Harper stood in front of Robert Payton's red door and knocked for the fourth time. She put her ear up to the door. No sound came from inside.

Her finger twitched on the trigger of her gun. She needed to put that away before she hurt someone, she thought. Her jumpiness about the man from the mall prevented her from obeying her thought, though. She would check the perimeter first then put away the gun.

Harri turned away from the door and took the stairs down to the main front walk. Robert Payton's home was a small one-story ranch-style house. The front yard was neat and trim, but the property wasn't eye-catching in any way. A nondescript house in a suburban neighborhood.

It was the perfect place to hide, she thought. She scanned the street to see if anyone was around. When she found it empty, Harri pushed through the box shrubs under the front window to the right of the front door and peeked inside.

By the furniture in the room, Harri guessed she was looking at his living room. She saw no signs of anyone being home. She struggled through the shrubs and returned to the front walk.

She checked the street.

Still no one around.

Harri walked quickly around the corner of the house onto the driveway. She was trespassing and wanted no nosy neighbors calling the police on her. Thankfully, the driveway had tall fir trees shielding it from the prying eyes of the neighbors on the right.

Her cheeks flushed. She still had her gun out.

Even better. A trespasser holding a gun.

She wouldn't make it out of this driveway alive if the neighbors called the cops. She put her gun back in her holster but kept her hand near it as she rounded the corner of the house.

A white panel van was parked in front of a small garage attached to the back of the house. It was a strange configuration for a garage. It did afford a certain amount of privacy for Robert Payton though. He'd have an easy time pulling the van up to the back of the house and depositing victims into the garage.

A footstep sounded behind her. Before Harri could pull her gun out, pain shot through her head. A thought floated into her consciousness as she sank into darkness.

How had he snuck up on her?

29

DAY 6 - NIGHT

Jake Tepesky met Gavin French at the home of Robert Payton. Jake had sped to the address, but Gavin beat him there. That was a good thing because Jake was about to pound down the door to find Harri. Gavin and two uniforms were walking down the drive away from the home. Without Harri.

"She's not there?" Jake asked, panic rising in his voice.

"There's no sign of her. We haven't found her car on the street, either."

"Did you talk to Payton?"

"No one home," Gavin said.

"She left me this address and told me she'd left the car at the high school."

Gavin's brow furrowed. "We told you to stay away from the Atticus Menlo case," he said.

Jake shook his head, confused. "We were. She was tracking down a lead on Dan Ledeyen's disappearance. What does this have to do with Atticus? Have you gotten ahold of the cameras at the mall?"

Jake had told him about the incident in the mall. Gavin was not happy to hear about the clothes found on Alan Prentiss.

"My men are on that. Why would she be at Atticus Menlo's school?"

So that's what the connection was, Jake thought.

"I don't know," Jake said. "Have you run a check on Robert Payton?"

Gavin nodded.

"He's a teacher at Milbourne High School."

"She didn't tell me what she was doing there. Something must have spooked her though since she texted me the address of where she was going. She's never done that before," Jake said.

He paced back and forth in the driveway, trying to discharge his heightened energy. Harri's disappearing was not good. Not good at all.

"Have you searched the property?"

"We have no reason to enter the property. We did look around the outside and we found nothing. No signs of a struggle."

"Should we go to the school? Check and see if her car is still there?" Jake asked.

"We can take my car since I have a radio. I'll leave the uniforms here in case Payton returns. They can hold him here until I get back. I'll question him about Harri, but we have to find him first."

Gavin turned to talk to the uniforms and when he was done, he waved Jake over. Jake joined him at the unmarked cruiser and got inside.

Harri was gone. Like Lauren. But Harri wasn't Lauren. She was a cop. She had skills.

Gavin clicked open the car locks.

"Hang in there, Harri," Jake muttered as he slid into

the passenger seat.

He clicked on his seatbelt and Gavin started the car.

"Milbourne High School is minutes away," Gavin said. "We'll find her."

Gavin didn't sound convincing.

Neither man spoke again until Gavin pulled into the visitor parking lot.

"That's her car," Jake pointed to the rental car.

It was the only car left in the lot.

"Do you have keys?" Gavin asked.

"No. There's only one set and they should be with Harri."

Gavin pulled up alongside the car and the two of them jumped out. Jake checked the driver's door. It was locked. He peered inside but the car was empty.

"She has her purse on her."

"I'm not seeing anything here," Gavin said.

"Me, neither."

Jake gritted his teeth. They couldn't just wait for her dead body to show up somewhere.

"We've been working on a theory," Jake began.

Gavin cocked his head at him, his mouth set in a thin line. He looked pissed.

"Which part of stay out of it did you two not understand?"

"We were staying away from your cases. This has directly to do with Lauren Harper's disappearance and also Dan Ledeyen's disappearance."

"And?" Gavin asked.

"There was a photo in Chris Becker's apartment. I saw it when we found his body."

"Right. The photo."

"Did you do anything with it yet?" Jake asked.

"We've been just a little bit busy finding dead boys in

the woods," Gavin said, frowning. Jake wondered if Gavin was thinking he'd missed something. Which he had.

"That camp in the photo with Lauren is connected to your case."

"How so?" Gavin asked.

"Lauren Harper was surrounded by eight boys at a camp during what appeared to be summer. She'd never been to Oregon before that September."

"Meaning?" Gavin asked.

"Meaning that photo had to be taken the summer after her disappearance."

"That's a terrible thought, but I'm not seeing the connection to my case," Gavin said.

"One of the boys in that photo was Chris Becker."

"Which would make sense that he had that photo, I guess," Gavin said.

His frown deepened.

"We think that's where the killer had been holding the boys," Jake said.

"You have evidence of this? That seems like a big jump."

"I'll explain my thought process as we're driving out there," Jake said.

"You found the camp?"

"Yes. I think that's where Dan Ledeyen is being held," Jake said.

"Why?"

"It's a hunch. I think the camp was a front for a child prostitution operation. It's where all of this started."

"Do you have any proof of this?"

"Not proof of the child prostitution ring. But it would be a perfect place to keep a victim. Especially if the perp was reliving some sort of fantasy or regression."

"And you know where the camp was located?"

"I have a map of it. Supposedly it's an hour away."

Gavin looked back at Harri's car.

"Lemme call this in and see what my LT says about it."

Jake nodded and watched Gavin walk away to make the phone call.

He kicked the wheel of the rental car in anger. He should have been her back up and he'd failed her. He would never do that again. Harri might be LAPD but every cop needed backup when they were in the crosshairs of a killer.

Gavin returned to the car. "We have the go-ahead. If we find anything out there, I'll make the call for support."

Jake nodded and they turned back to the unmarked cruiser.

I'm coming, Harri. Hang in there. We're coming.

30

DAY 6 - NIGHT

Harri Harper woke up groaning and grabbed her head. She felt nothing wet which was good. At least he hadn't cracked her skull when he'd taken her, but she was sure she had a concussion.

When she moved, nausea filled her mouth and her eyes blurred. Definitely a concussion.

A barely lit bulb gave the room a sickly yellow glow. Harri wiped at her eyes and worked hard on focusing. Whoever had taken her had left her in what appeared to be a basement room. A turned-over desk and several chairs were piled in a corner. Otherwise, the room was empty. There were no windows on any of the walls. The only way out looked to be a door. She was sure it was locked from the outside.

Harri shifted and the pain in her head almost sent her back into unconsciousness. She knew from her training that her best bet was to escape. No way was her abductor going to let her go. Of that, she was certain.

Harri forced herself to her feet, her head splitting in pain from the movement, and shuffled towards the door.

The room shifted beneath her as her body sent out signals for her to stop moving.

She shuffled further.

Tears streamed down her face as she reached the door and tried the knob. It was locked as she'd assumed. Harri slipped back down to the ground. Her stillness allowed the pain in her head to momentarily subside. She scanned her surroundings again.

The only opening she saw was a small air vent in the ceiling. Could she fit through that? She listened for any evidence of her abductor being nearby. The place was completely silent.

How long had she been here? She pulled up her sleeve and checked her smartwatch. Her abductor hadn't taken that from her, at least. It had been about four hours since she'd been at Robert Payton's house.

Harri grappled with her situation.

She had seen no one at Payton's house.

Did Robert Payton take her?

Could she be in his converted garage?

If that was the case, she'd already have been found. Jake had Robert Payton's address and he must know by now she'd been taken. Knowing him, he'd have contacted Gavin French and they'd have searched Payton's property. That means whoever took her had moved her. That didn't bode well for her chances of survival. She had to find a way out of here.

Harri tried to get back on her feet and groaned again with the effort. Her head pounded as she stood swaying. She shook the dizziness off as her hand searched for her weapon belt under her arm. Of course, he'd taken her gun.

Her gun.

Oh god, that was bad.

A cop's service weapon out in the wild. Crap.

She had lost her weapon and she'd let herself be taken.

What a fool she'd been to go on her own. Her judgment had been reckless in this case. She should have waited for Jake. Her gut had told her something was off. This case made her do too many dangerous things and now here she was.

Her breath caught in her chest as fear cascaded through her. This was not the time to freeze. Harri gritted her teeth.

She needed to act. She was a professional. She'd been taken and she needed out. This was not the way she would go down.

Her eyes drifted to the air filter. Outside of the door, that was the only other opening. She moved again and this time the nausea overwhelmed her. She dry-heaved but nothing much came out. She had eaten little over the last day. Small mercies, she supposed.

She attempted to move again. Her vision blurred and she sank back down to the ground. Darkness crowded on the edges of her vision. She was losing consciousness.

She just needed to sleep.

If she slept for a little bit, her head would be better.

Harri folded into herself and let the blackness take over. At least, she wouldn't feel the pain in her head.

31

DAY 6 - NIGHT

Richard Miller looked over his map and shone his flashlight on the path that was barely there. He'd dug out the old map from twenty-five years ago. He'd saved it just in case something like this happened.

He knew that what he would find there might destroy his life. But if he could save just one boy, then he had to do it. He hadn't been able to do it twenty-five years ago. All he'd managed to do was save himself and Bobby.

"I'm not going into that water, Rich," Bobby said, his teeth chattering. They'd heard the shots and ran as fast as they could to the water's edge.

"They'll kill us otherwise," Rich said. He waded into the water and shivered from the cold. The air around them was warm but the water wasn't. He faintly remembered something about not swimming in too cold water because you'd fall asleep or something. They didn't have another choice.

Rich yanked Bobby by the arm. "Do you know how to swim?"

Bobby nodded. He shot a look behind them.

"They're coming," Bobby said.

Rich yanked him harder. "Swim now!" he hissed. He shoved Bobby in.

Bobby gasped from the cold.

"Swim," Rich said again. He dived in next to him.

The cold slammed against his body. His eyes widened and he gasped.

Swim, his inner voice commanded.

Bobby had started doing the crawl next to him. Rich pulled his arm out of the water and forced his body to do the same movement as Bobby.

He didn't know how they'd survive this swim, but it was better than what was waiting for them on that island.

They had escaped. Swam through the freezing water to get to the other side of the lake. To freedom.

He and Bobby had luck on their side that night. The temperature had been warm still and the water wasn't cold enough for full-on hypothermia to set in. He'd swore that night he'd never come back to these woods.

And yet here he was. Back in these same woods. He thought he'd left all this behind. He did everything he could to forget about that summer. He'd created a family for himself and did his best to take care of them. He knew he'd never be able to make amends for the boys he'd left behind. The boys and Lauren Harper.

His terror that night shamed him. His therapist reminded him that he'd been just a boy himself. The shame remained, nonetheless. He would set things right this time even if he lost his life doing it. He owed the ones he'd left behind.

He was okay with that.

He just had to find the damn place.

Richard picked his way through the overgrown path, his backpack bumping along on his back. The flashlight he'd brought kept flickering. Richie must have been playing with it again. Pain shot through his chest. He'd never see his boy again. And his sweet wife. Maybe he should have called the cops on Bobby. He gnawed on his lip. He had no proof, and a boy was still missing.

Bobby was the one taking the boys, of that he was sure. Bobby hadn't been able to move on from that time. He didn't get the life he thought he deserved. The man was filled with rage.

Rage at what had happened to him. What happened to them all.

The last time they'd met, Richard saw the rage and tried to ignore it. He offered his therapist's information. Suggested he might want to get help. Bobby said he was just fine.

He wanted to help him. They'd survived that place together. They were the only ones who understood what really happened there. Everyone else died. He hadn't wanted to think Bobby had become as twisted and horrible as the men who'd abused them. He'd been so wrong.

Now he was the only one who could stop Bobby. Stop him at the place where it all started.

Richard had given his son and his wife kisses goodbye. His wife begged him not to go. He'd never told her what happened. She guessed bits and pieces of it, though. He promised her he'd be back. It was the first time he'd ever lied to her.

The only other thing she'd asked of him was to make it back home. He lied to her and promised he would.

He doubted he'd make it out of the forest. Really, he'd been there all these years anyway.

He told her he loved her and squeezed his son. He'd kept it together until he reached his car. There he lost it and sobbed all the way to the forest.

Now that he was here, his nightmares had become his reality. The trees felt as if they were closing in all around him. Every noise that filtered through the dark forest made his heart jump. He'd not been back in the woods since that night.

Despite the fear that gripped his heart, Richard kept on walking. He'd loved the quiet nature of these woods when he was little. Camping was one of his favorite things, one of the few joys of his bleak existence. It was the reason he'd been so excited to go to the camp in the first place.

Little did he know he'd agreed to go to a hell he wouldn't be able to escape. He sucked in his breath.

A sob caught in his throat and he choked on it.

Of course, he'd have a panic attack here. It was fitting. He was in his own personal hell, after all.

He'd suffered from them ever since that night, he'd eventually been pretty good at controlling them. Tonight though, he doubted he'd be so successful. He might die tonight, and he was willing to do so.

A stick cracked somewhere off in the distance and he froze. His breath was ragged as tears streamed down his cheeks.

He sprinted forward; roots be damned. He had to get to that island and now. The faster he got out of these woods, the quicker he'd be able to get up enough courage to do what he had to do.

Kill the man he'd escaped with. Find the boy he'd taken. Save someone from that dark place.

Richard ran out of the forest and onto the small rocky beach. He stopped to catch his breath. The lake looked just like it had that night. He didn't need his flashlight anymore and put it away. A full moon hung over the lake making the night unnaturally bright.

He scanned the shore. Bobby would need a boat to get onto the other side. He spotted a bright flash of metal and ran over to the large bushes hoping there was a boat hidden underneath there.

Richard pulled the branches away and found a rowboat. It was new. He'd been right about Bobby coming back here.

32

DAY 6 - NIGHT

Harri woke up sprawled against the door of her prison. Her head still throbbed but when she moved nausea didn't overwhelm her. That was a big step forward. She checked her watch again and swore. The battery had died.

She put her ear to the door and listened. Still no sound coming from the other side. She had to move now. Harri pulled herself up and swallowed down the vomit that raced up her throat. She fought through the dizziness and walked over to the air vent. It looked impossibly small. She might be able to wiggle through if she could get up there. Her attention shifted to the desk and chairs.

If they were stacked up, she'd reach the ceiling, no problem. She dragged the desk right underneath the air vent. By her estimation, she still wouldn't be able to reach high enough to pull herself through. Harri set one of the chairs on top of the desk. That would give her enough height to be able to open it, she thought.

She breathed deep and steadied herself by holding

onto the desk. Hopefully, she didn't topple from this tower of hers and hurt her head even worse. She looked back at the ceiling.

How was she going to get that air vent cover off? Typically, she would use a screwdriver. What did she have on her with a small enough edge? She peered around the room but nothing like that stood out to her. She patted herself down and felt something in her jean pocket. Triumphantly, she pulled a penny out of her pocket. She held it up in ecstasy.

The penny gave her the adrenaline she needed to clamber up on that desk. The desk wiggled beneath her. Or was that her head? Undaunted, she climbed up on the chair and steadied herself before attempting to stand. She waited and gained her bearings and then stood on wobbly feet.

To her relief, the desk and chair gave her enough height to reach the air duct and pull herself through it. The problem was she couldn't stand upright. Unscrewing the air duct cover would be challenging.

Harri shifted to the left and used the penny to start on the first screw. She twisted the penny around, and the screw came loose. Her back was cramping up, but she kept on. The next two screws came out without a hitch but the fourth refused to budge. The screw itself was damaged and rusty. She couldn't even get the penny into the groove.

She tugged on the free edges of the cover. The one corner didn't budge.

Harri bit her lip. She was so close.

She tugged it again and the chair, with her on it, swayed back and forth. Crap, she thought. The floor looked far away suddenly, and she focused back up on her cover.

What if, she thought and bent the cover all the way back as far as it could go. That would be enough to get her through. One barrier down.

Next was getting herself in there.

She repositioned her body under the air duct and put her arms up. She slowly straightened while using her arms to maneuver herself into the duct. Once she was halfway in, she pressed hard against the duct walls and inched the rest of her body into it. By the time her entire body was inside, she was sweating profusely, and her head was spinning. Her breathing was ragged and coming out in short puffs.

The dust inside was thick and she sneezed several times as she inched forward. She felt like a worm. She heard a sound come from somewhere ahead of her. She worked her way through the duct faster.

For what seemed like an eternity she wiggled and scrunched and wiggled and scrunched until she found a corner. It was dark and dusty, and she didn't even want to think about the material she was crawling into, but she kept thinking of the boys that had been found. She thought of what happened to them and she kept on going.

She felt something scuttle across her arm and bit back a cry. She didn't mind bugs, but she really hated spiders. The thought of how many spiders could be crawling through this duct made her involuntarily twitch. She bit her lip hard and tried not to shriek in fear.

Focus, she thought and wiggled forward. She kept up her pace until she hit a corner. She maneuvered around it and was relieved to feel the duct around her grow bigger. This would enable her to move faster.

Harri used her arms to pull herself forward. She felt

like she'd crossed several rooms when she heard crying. A child crying.

No, someone older. A boy, maybe. Or someone about to become a teenager. She pushed her body harder and focused on where the crying was coming from. It occurred to her the crying boy could be Dan Ledeyen.

Nausea came up again and she swallowed it back. She was so close. She squeezed her eyes shut and breathed the stale air in and out. In and out. She opened her eyes again even though all she could see was black. The crying was getting closer. She crawled again.

She kept moving until the sound of the crying boy was right below her. The problem was that she was encased in a metal duct and had no idea how she would get out of it. Her fingers searched for a seam or an opening. Her forward momentum slowed as her fingers searched for another air duct.

Several feet further and she found the grooves she was looking for. There was no light coming from below. She had no idea how to get the screws off. Harri pushed hard at the air vent cover below her.

She pushed harder.

Crack.

CRRRRACK.

Harri felt the rush of air as she fell out of the duct.

Pain screamed through her shoulder as it hit the dirt floor. She cried out as she lay there, broken and bruised. She tried to move, but the pain in her collarbone was intense. She'd broken it, she was sure. The ceiling had cushioned her fall somewhat and she hadn't hit her head. Small battles won, she thought.

She pulled herself up and whimpered. It hurt so damn much. A smell of feces and urine hit her nose, hard. She gagged at how bad the stench was.

"Who are you?" A boy's voice came from somewhere in the distance.

"My name is..." Harri struggled to find her voice. "My name is Harri Harper. I'm a detective."

"I know you. You come to see my dad every year," the young boy said.

"Dan Ledeyen?" she asked.

"Yeah, that's me."

She had finally found Dan Ledeyen and he was still alive.

"I've been looking for you. Since you disappeared. Your parents are going to be so happy that we found you alive."

"Alan didn't make it, did he?" Dan asked.

"Why would you ask that?" she asked.

"I heard him mouthing off to Bobby. You can't mouth off to Bobby because he gets angry. And when he gets angry, he does bad things," he said, his voice low.

"Robert Payton is the one who abducted you?" Harri asked.

"Yeah. He grabbed me after my job interview at Starbucks. He called out to me, said he needed to talk to me about class. I got close to his car and he had a gun. He made me get in his car." His voice was closer to Harri.

He'd crawled over to her, but she couldn't see him because they were in total darkness.

"Have you been here the entire time?"

"I was in his trunk for a while. He drugged me when he opened the trunk door. I woke up here."

"How did you know Alan was here?" she asked.

"He was in the next room. He started yelling and screaming and that's when I heard Bobby go crazy on him."

"How come you didn't go crazy in front of him?" Harri asked.

"Because I'd seen him get angry before."

"Here?"

"No. In class. I knew better than to set him off like that," he said.

"Good thing you did."

Harri sat cradling her arm, trying to breathe normally.

"We gotta get out of here," she said.

Harri sat up and gritted her teeth against the pain.

"I think I broke something," she said.

"Your arm?" Dan asked.

"My collarbone," she said. "I also have a concussion."

"He's coming back tonight. I heard him talking to himself," he said.

"That doesn't give us a lot of time. He's gonna be upset when he finds out I escaped out of my room," she said.

"How did you get out?" he asked.

"I found an air conditioning vent in the ceiling. I don't think he meant to take me," she added. She felt the boy at her side.

"Thank you for trying to find me," he said.

With that, he broke down. Dan burrowed into her side, his body shaking from silent sobs. Harri winced because of the pain but let him hide his face.

She'd seen what waited for him. For both of them.

She steeled herself for what was to come next.

33

DAY 6 - NIGHT

Jake held onto the car door as Detective Gavin French raced towards the coordinates that Dr. Brand had written down on the map. Their headlights illuminated the forest on either side of them. As the scenery rushed by, Jake felt as if the trees were closing in on them, following them and waiting to swallow them whole. His thoughts had turned dark and desperate as they barreled towards what Jake hoped would be the correct camp.

His discussion with Dr. Brand about the viability of the location had been sound. But with Harri's life on the line, Jake was having a hard time not doubting himself.

"We're about ten minutes out," Gavin said.

They'd spoken little on the ride. Jake bounced his knee up and down throughout his time in the car and he'd noticed Gavin watching the movement.

"I should have been with her," Jake said.

"Why weren't you with her? I thought both of you were searching for Dan?"

Jake clenched his fist in response. He'd made a

terrible decision in splitting up.

"I was working the Chris Becker camp angle. She was working the Dan case."

Gavin hit his wheel. "Aha. I knew it. Didn't we tell you to stay away from that?"

"Yes. And to be fair, I had no desire to investigate who killed Chris Becker. Special Agent McNarin made it quite clear there'd be hell to pay if we got muddled into that."

"All you were doing was ..." Gavin waved his hand for Jake to keep talking.

"The photo. Find all the boys in it to talk with them about what happened back then. And finding its location. I think even you would agree we were doing a good job of staying away from your cases."

"Then why grab Harri?" Gavin asked.

Jake had been wondering the same thing. "With the break-ins at the Inn, we assumed someone was warning us off."

"I'm sure that only emboldened Harri to keep going," Gavin remarked.

A fleeting smile crossed his face.

"You know her so well," Jake said.

"Well enough. The only other explanation is that Harri became a target. But for who?"

"The victim profile doesn't match, obviously. I don't know why a man with the kind of fantasy life of your killer would want anything to do with a forty-something cop."

"Unless she uncovered his secret," Gavin reminded him.

"You're thinking she caught Robert Payton in mid-murder or kidnapping and he had to grab her for that?"

"When you say it like that, it doesn't make much

sense," Gavin said.

"It would be hard to control a teenage boy and a cop," Jake said.

Jake's phone beeped with directions to the coordinates.

"Turn off here." Jake pointed left to a dirt road barely visible in the headlights.

Gavin slammed on the brakes and the cruiser squeaked as they made the turn.

"A little bit more notice next time," Gavin grumbled.

"It's this unpaved road all the way to the small lot," Jake said.

The branches of the trees scratched against the exterior of the car making a sound like nails on a chalkboard. Jake's skin crawled from the sound.

"I'm still not entirely sold on this theory of yours," Gavin said.

"I appreciate your coming out here with me then."

"I don't want to find any more dead bodies on this case," Gavin said. "Truth be told, we've hit dead ends on both of those boys. All the pedos we called in had alibis of some sort or another. The feds grabbed the Chris Becker child porn case."

"What about Blue and Peanut? Anything come up about them?" Jake asked.

Jake had told Gavin about the information Harri had gleaned from Thomas James about what the boys did for money. Gavin hadn't been too surprised and had put the names in as aliases of potential pedos. Jake had been taken off the case before any of that investigation had started.

"None of the pedos we brought claimed to know those two. I didn't believe some of them, but we couldn't crack them. That ended up dead-ending."

"Harri was looking for Thomas James. He was an addict in rehab with Dan Ledeyen. He checked himself out after speaking with Harri. He sounded like he had dealings with this crew. You might want to try tracking him down," Jake suggested.

"I'll put that in the case-file," Gavin said.

"Are you thinking Dan might be connected now?" Jake asked.

"Don't you?" Gavin asked as the narrow drive opened to a small field.

"I don't know how to answer that. If I say yes, we'll be closed out of the case again," Jake said.

Gavin had no reply for that. He eased the cruiser into the small field.

"This looks like a landing area," Gavin said.

"The expert told me it would look something like this. I guess we're here."

Jake looked out into the darkness. A full moon was rising in the sky and bathed the surroundings in a pale blue light. It would have been beautiful under different circumstances. Tonight, it appeared sinister and deadly.

"She said we had about a fifteen-minute hike to the lake. Supposedly the camp is on an island in the middle of the lake," Jake said.

"How the hell are we supposed to get on an island?" grumbled Gavin.

A lump jumped into Jake's throat. If Harri was out here somewhere, how in the hell were they going to find her? The area around them was vast.

Not for the first time this evening, a cold bead of sweat ran down his forehead. Fear gripped his throat, and he couldn't open his mouth.

He wasn't sure they would succeed tonight.

34

DAY 6 - NIGHT

Dan Ledeyen helped Harri move as far away from the door as they could get. They huddled in the corner together, making sure they kept their voices low. Harri knew that once Robert Payton found her missing, he'd come to check in on Dan immediately.

They needed a plan.

"Have you searched for any escape routes?" Harri asked, keeping her voice low.

"I've searched and searched and there's no way to get up to the ceiling like you did because there's no furniture in the room. There's only the door and he's got a lock on it."

"How often does he come? How does he bring you water and food? What's the schedule like?" she asked.

"I don't know. I don't have a watch or a phone. I can't figure out time anymore. I don't know if it's day or night, or what. I'll be starving and thirsty when he comes so I guess there are hours between the visits. He gives me bologna sandwiches and two water bottles to drink. By the time he's back, I'm out of both."

"When was the last time you saw him?" she asked.

"It hasn't been that long. I still have one bottle of water left and I'm not hungry. I've been here long enough that I get confused, though. I wouldn't put too much stock into any of my impressions. He's kept me in the dark the entire time, too. My senses are all whack. When did he grab you?" Dan asked.

"He grabbed me in the afternoon," Harri said. "My smartwatch was working back in the other room. I'd only been here a few hours when I woke up the first time. I passed out again and my watch died, so I have no idea about time now, either."

The kid had pulled himself together and had pulled away from Harri. Good, Harri thought. She knew her presence there gave him hope even though at the moment she was just as much of a prisoner as he was.

"There's two of us now. When he does come in, we can use the element of surprise to overpower him," Harri said.

"He's too big. Strong," Dan said. "He's way bigger than me. I can't take him. And you're hurt."

"He still won't be expecting the two of us in here. That must count for something," Harri replied.

"Sure, okay." Dan didn't sound convinced.

"We ARE getting out of here, Dan," Harri said.

"Have you talked to my mom and dad?" Dan asked.

She heard hope in his voice, laced with sadness. A sound made Harri put her hand on his arm to stop him from talking.

"Do you hear him approaching?"

They both remained still in the silent darkness.

"Yes," Dan whispered. "There's three locks on the door. It takes him a while to open them all."

"That will buy us some time. We need to get in position."

Harri hoped they could aim for his feet and topple him. If she could get their abductor in a chokehold, he'd pass out and they'd have a chance.

"So, I should be at the door?" Dan asked.

"Yes," Harri whispered. "Go for his feet and topple him. I'll get him in a chokehold."

"What about your collarbone?" Dan asked.

"The chokehold is more about positioning than force."

"Maybe you could show me, and I could do it on him."

Harri wished they had light to do just that. But in the pitch-dark, it was no use.

"It's the best we have right now. Without light, I can't show you the right positioning." Harri explained.

"I don't want to die here," Dan whispered.

"Neither do I," Harri agreed. "We have to do something. He's going to kill us otherwise. I'd rather be in pain than dead."

Dan said nothing for a moment.

"What did he do to Alan?"

Harri thought briefly that she should lie to him, to keep his hopes up. She couldn't do it. He needed to know exactly the danger they were in.

"Killed him," Harri told him. "He was found in the woods yesterday."

"Man," Dan said with a catch in his voice. "Oh, Man. He had a lot of problems, but he didn't deserve to die."

"No, he didn't," Harri said as gently as she could.

"That's not going to happen to us though, right? We're together now and we're gonna fight. Right, Dan?"

She waited in the darkness for Dan's agreement.

"Yeah," he said softly with conviction. "Yeah, let's fight this sick fucker."

"Alright," Harri instructed. "I'll wait on the side of the door that will be hidden when he opens it. You go on the side of the doorknob."

Harri dragged herself by touch along the wall until she felt the door and went up on her knees to feel the doorknob. The doorknob was on the left which meant the door would swing out towards the right. That's where she would wait.

Dan was right behind her. When she took her position, he pushed past her. She heard him fiddle with the doorknob and then settle.

"As soon as he's in, you go for his legs, okay?"

"Got it," Dan said. "Let's take him down."

Now all they could do was wait.

Harri sat there, breathing through her radiating pain. Dan sniffled in the darkness. Finally, a door creaked open somewhere in the distance.

"Did you hear that?" Dan whispered.

"Get ready, Dan." She whispered back. "We only have one shot at this."

"Wait," Dan said. "He doesn't sound right."

"What do you mean?" Harri asked, still whispering.

"The sound of his walking. It doesn't sound right. He shuffles."

The footsteps became loud and clear from the other side of the door. The person on the other end was definitely not shuffling.

"Have you ever seen anyone else here?" she asked.

"No. Just Bobby," Dan replied. "This doesn't sound like him."

Harri held her breath as a lock clicked open on the other side.

Two more to go.

The doorknob rattled.

"Get ready," Harri hissed.

The doorknob rattled harder.

"It's not him," Dan said in a panic. "He has keys. Whoever's out there doesn't have the keys."

A glimmer of hope sprung in Harri. Maybe, they'd get out alive after all.

Harri banged on the door.

"We're in here," she shouted. "Hey, we're in here!"

"Hey," Dan banged on the door. "Get us out!"

"I hear you. Get away from the door. I'm going to have to break it down," the voice said from the other side of the door.

Harri dragged herself to the left. Something heavy banged on the other side. A yelp of pain and a grunt came from the other side.

The door wasn't budging.

Silence. Please don't give up, Harri thought.

A scraping sound came from the edge of the door. A pop and then the scraping again. Another bang and then finally, thank god, the door swung open.

A man's silhouette filled the doorway. The moonlight shone so brightly that Harri had to cover her eyes.

"Hello?" A man's voice filled the darkness. "My name's Richard. I'm here to help," the voice said. "Who's in here?"

"Harri, I'm a cop," Harri replied.

She pushed against the wall to get on her feet. She

flinched with every movement as her collarbone screamed in pain and her head throbbed.

Dan stepped out into the moonlight. "I'm Dan Ledeyen. Robert Payton abducted me."

"We gotta get outta here," Harri said. "Bobby will be back soon."

The man named Richard grimaced.

"Bobby took you?"

Dan nodded.

"Damn. I'm sorry I didn't get here sooner. Should have known," Richard shook his head. "I should have known."

"How did you know where to find us?" Harri asked as Richard helped her to her feet.

He scanned the cramped space with his flashlight before they all left the room and started down the small hallway.

"I escaped from this place with Bobby close to twenty-five years ago," Richard explained. "I think we're the only ones left that know about it. Besides them, of course. The ones who set it all up."

Harri had so many questions she couldn't ask. They had to get out of here first. Escape and survive. Get Dan out safe. Then she could ask all the questions tumbling through her mind. What about Lauren? No, she had to wait. She pushed thoughts of Lauren back into the recesses of her mind.

"You saved us, Richard. Thank you." She attempted to lift her arm and winced.

"Did you break your arm?" he asked.

"My collarbone. I won't be able to move too fast. Where are we?"

"We're in the middle of the Willamette Forest. On an island actually."

"Island?" Harri knew there was no way in hell she'd be able to swim.

"What?" Dan asked in confusion. "How did he get us out here?"

"Did he break it?" Richard asked, his voice shaking with anger.

"No. I fell out of the ceiling as I was escaping," she said.

They emerged out of the small building into an overgrown clearing. The full moon provided enough light to allow them to see where to go. The water glimmered in the moonlight behind the trees in front of them.

"What time is it?" she asked.

"Ten-thirty," Richard answered. "Bobby wasn't home. That's why I came here to find him. He must be on his way."

Harri's mind raced. She was sure Richard was right. The killer must be on his way back to their location. They had to move fast.

"You have a phone on you?" Harri asked.

"Yeah, but it won't do us any good out here. No service," Richard said.

He showed her the phone face. No reception.

"How did you get here?" Dan asked.

"I found his boat hidden in some bushes," Richard said.

Something alerted within in Harri's mind.

"How did you know where to look?"

"Bobby had to get out here somehow," Richard explained as they walked. "When we escaped, we had to swim in the cold water and almost died from hypothermia. I knew he'd have a boat stashed."

Harri stumbled on a root. She gasped as pain shot

through her body. She couldn't figure out which was worse, her head or her collarbone.

Their little group emerged onto a small, rocky beach. A metal rowboat rocked against the gentle waves of the lake. Harri bit her lip as she scanned the distant shore. They would be sitting ducks in that boat.

"Bobby will be looking for his boat. He'll be coming to the landing where you found it. What if we row to the other side?" Harri asked.

Richard thought for a moment, then shook his head. "I don't know of any trails leading out of the forest on that side. We'll be lost in the woods without any supplies. I only have one bottle of water."

Harri nodded as Richard helped Dan into the boat. She held out her arm and Richard steadied her as she clambered in behind Dan. The adrenaline that kept her walking also made her jumpy. As much as Harri wanted to get Dan and herself off the island, she did not want to be in this boat.

Richard waded into the water, pushing the boat out. The boat bottom grated against the lake floor and then floated. Richard held the boat steady as he climbed inside.

He took the oars and expertly maneuvered the boat towards the distant shore.

She looked over at Dan. He was quiet, but she could see his shoulders shaking as he tried to hold himself together. His breath was ragged, and she knew it was from the tears he was holding in.

Harri couldn't wait any longer. She wasn't sure she should ask her questions around Dan, but she also wasn't sure he was even listening to them, either.

"You were one of the kids here? The abused kids?" Harri asked.

Richard nodded without saying anything. Dan shifted behind her, burying his face in his hands.

"Did you know my sister Lauren Harper?" Harri asked.

"I did." Richard nodded slowly.

Harri's heart leaped into her throat.

"D…d..id…what happened to her?" Harri got out.

"She's dead. They killed her that night. With the others," Richard said in short staccato words.

"Where…who?" Harri asked, her head throbbing as her heart raced. She needed to calm herself down.

"She's buried on the island along with the six other boys." His voice turned husky and cracked as he finished the sentence.

"Who killed them?" Harri asked.

"The men that came in the night. I only heard their voices. They never used their names," Richard said.

"Did you see them die?" Dan's question surprised her.

"Through the bushes. Me and Bobby made a run for it. We hid while the others ran the other direction. They picked them off one by one."

Her sister died on that island and her body was buried there. Somewhere.

"Who brought you to this camp?" she asked.

"It was supposed to be a wilderness camp for troubled teens. My foster parents sent me there," Richard said and laughed harshly.

"Why didn't the missing kids get reported?"

"We were foster kids. Street kids. Throwaways," Richard replied bitterly. "It was a whole racket," Richard said as they reached the other shore.

His breathing came out harsh and ragged. The

rowing had taken a toll on him as his face trickled with sweat.

"We..."

Before he could say anything else, the sound of a pop carried over the lake.

It was the unmistakable sound of a gunshot.

"Down. Everyone down," Harri yelled.

35

DAY 6 - NIGHT

Jake and Gavin fished their backpacks out of the back seat. Gavin checked his weapon as Jake spread the map on the hood of the car. He peered at the circled area that Dr. Brand had shown him. She'd drawn in a trail that started on the north side of the small field.

Jake shone his flashlight at the trees while checking the compass on his phone. He noted there was no cell service out here. Jake turned due north and moved the flashlight beam along the bottoms of the trees looking for an opening.

"Searching for the path?" Gavin asked.

"Yeah. We're going to have to get closer to find it. My contact told me it's a path not many people know about and might look like one of those animal trails."

"Great," Gavin muttered.

"At least, we have the moon," Jake offered.

"We won't, once we enter the woods," Gavin said.

"I checked the reception here. We don't have any..."

Before Jake could finish, the unmistakable POP POP of gunfire sounded in the distance.

Both men fell to the ground, taking cover.

"Those were definitely gunshots," Jake said. "Is there night hunting around here?"

"No. I'm calling this in," Gavin said.

He kept his body low as he moved to the driver's side of the cruiser and used the hand radio to call in for back-up. As he read out the coordinates to dispatch, Jake kept shining his beam of light onto the trees, searching for the trail.

Harri was out there somewhere, he was sure of that now. He hoped the gunfire was Harri's and not someone shooting at her.

His flashlight found a small opening around the middle of what appeared to be an impenetrable wall of fir trees.

"I think I found it. The trail," Jake said as Gavin returned, shotgun by his side.

"My men are twenty minutes out," he said. "I've asked for air assist, too. We might need a ride to that island."

Pop.

Pop.

More gunshots rang out.

"Let's go," Jake said and took off towards the mouth of the trail, Gavin running right behind him.

36

DAY 6 - NIGHT

Harri lay in the bottom of the boat as the shots pinged all around. Richard's face was close to hers as Dan lay whimpering in a tight ball at her feet.

"We can't stay here," Harri said to him.

"Should we try our chances on the shore?" Richard asked.

"We don't know his location and he has the advantage of tree coverage," Harri said. "He'll be able to take us out as we get off the boat."

"Then back to the island?" Richard asked.

"What about the other side?" Harri asked.

"He'll be able to reach us there, but it's a long hike. Without a boat, he won't be able to get to us. He won't swim out there. The water is too cold. I know Bobby."

Another bullet pinged off the metal of the boat.

"Whatever we do, we have to do it now."

Richard nodded and lifted his arm to the oar still attached to the boat.

"I'll try to push us out."

He maneuvered the oar to the bottom of the lake. It scraped the rocks beneath them and Harri felt the boat gently push away from the shore.

"How far will we need to go to be out of range?" Richard asked.

"I don't know what kind of gun he's using. It doesn't sound like a rifle, though." Harri said.

"Okay then," Richard said and sat up.

"What are you doing?" Harri exclaimed.

"Getting us out of here," Richard said.

Another gunshot whizzed by them. Richard doubled down on his effort to row. He blanched as he pushed and pulled and pushed and pulled. The boat was gaining speed. Harri peeked out over the boat's side to see if she could see where Robert Payton was shooting from.

The beach looked empty.

Another shot rang out over the lake, but Robert's aim wasn't good. She didn't hear the whizz as the bullet shot through the air.

"I think we've gotten out of range," Harri said. She turned to look at Dan. "It's okay to get up now Dan."

He nodded but stayed curled up in a ball.

Harri left him like that and turned back to Richard.

"Did you see Robert?"

Richard shook his head.

"No," he said. "The sound bouncing around the lake isn't helpful, either."

"No movement in the trees?"

"Too dark," Richard said.

"We can stay on the island until morning," Harri said.

And then what, she thought. She wasn't convinced the island would be a sanctuary like Richard seemed to think. What if Robert Payton did decide to swim? None of them had a gun. They'd be stuck. Or they could take the boat out again. They just had to survive until morning. Then their options improved.

Harri winced as the pain in her body overwhelmed all her defenses. She gritted her teeth. She would be okay.

They would be okay.

37

DAY 6 - NIGHT

Jake and Gavin crashed through the low underbrush and took off down the barely visible trail. Gavin took the lead, his arms pumping, the shotgun swinging too close for Jake's liking. Jake was right behind him, his Glock in hand. Within minutes, Jake's breathing turned ragged. Gavin was obviously a runner and Jake was having difficulty keeping pace. As Gavin sped up, so did he. He would not be left behind in these woods.

Jake's senses were firing on all cylinders.

Every single crack made his heart jump.

Every sound that came from the darkness around them made him involuntarily duck his head. He could barely see where he was going and trusted that Gavin was staying on course. The path beneath them was very faint and resembled more of an animal track than a proper hiking trail.

Tree roots jutting out of the ground made it impossible to run without constantly checking the trail. Gavin stumbled on one and Jake grabbed him hard so he wouldn't topple over.

"How much longer do you think," he hissed to Gavin.

Up to that point, Gavin had been doing a decent job of going around roots and not flinching at every sound that emanated from the woods. Until he almost ate it. Jake didn't know what would have happened to that shotgun if he had.

"I think we're close. I can see the moon reflecting on the water over there," Gavin said pointing in the distance.

The man was barely breathing hard. Jake promised himself that if he got out of this alive, he would start running again.

"Here we are, here we are," Gavin ground to a halt at the edge of a small beach.

He pointed to a large lake illuminated by the full moon with a small island right in the middle of it.

"How are we going to get there?" Jake asked.

A gunshot sounded in the direction of the island and the sound bounced around the big lake.

"The action is over there," Jake said. "Harri and Dan must be on that island."

"We gotta figure out some way to get out there," Gavin said. He checked the time on his phone. "Backup isn't arriving for another ten minutes, at least."

"They could be dead by then," Jake said grimly.

"I know," Gavin said.

"Should we swim for it?" Jake asked.

"Do you know how cold that water must be?"

"Too cold to make it to the other side?" Jake guessed.

He knew water under 70 degrees Fahrenheit was too cold to be in for very long. And even if he was experienced at cold water swimming, which he wasn't, he also wasn't in the best shape, as evidenced by his sprinting.

"We can't swim," Gavin shook his head.

"How did they get out there?" Jake asked.

"Had to have a boat somewhere," Gavin said.

The full moon hung over the lake. Between the reflections and the ambient light, the open area was surprisingly light.

"There," Jake said pointing. "See the metal. There's our boat." The small boat was sitting on the rocky beach of the island.

"That's not helpful," Gavin said.

Thump Thump Thump.

The distant sound of a helicopter got louder and louder.

"The cavalry is early," Gavin said.

38

DAY 6 - NIGHT

"We can get out now," Harri tried again.

Dan Ledeyen sobbed at the bottom of the boat. The boy's fear overwhelmed him, and he couldn't move.

Richard tried next.

"We'll be safer amongst the trees. I know you think you're safe, but the beach is out in the open."

Dan lowered his arm away from his face. He had dark circles under his eyes and his skin looked waxen, with a sheen of sweat reflecting the moonlight. He was in shock.

"Dan, you need to walk. It's not good for your heart to be scrunched like that," Harri said.

His body unfurled and he sat up. His gaze shifted to the faraway beach.

"Is he there?"

"We have a whole body of water between us," Harri said although she wasn't sure that was the case. "Let's take cover."

She offered her hand, and he took it.

"I don't want to go back to that building," Dan whispered.

"It'll be warmer there," Richard said.

Harri noticed that he was shaking.

"We can go to another part of the structure, but we should get inside. Richard, will you lead us?"

"If I can remember," he said.

He led them through the trees. Harri couldn't make out any discernible path, but that didn't mean there wasn't one. Dan walked silently next to her, sniffling off and on.

"We're going to make it out of here," Harri whispered to him.

"How can you be sure of that?"

Her eyes met Dan's. His eyes were wide, and he wasn't blinking.

"Because we're survivors. All three of us," Harri reassured him. "Because I told your mom and dad that I would bring you home, and I will. Because Richard is a survivor and he found us. Because you stayed clean after rehab, which means you want to get better. You want to survive. So, we are all getting out of here alive."

Dan nodded his head. "You almost have me believing you." His voice came out low, barely a whisper.

"Believe me." She squeezed his hand in encouragement.

"Over here," Richard's voice called out ahead of them.

By stopping and speaking, Harri and Dan had fallen behind. The trees were dense, and the moon didn't filter through much. They'd been walking in very dim light and with Harri's pain, very slowly.

"Where are you?" Harri called out.

"Over here," Richard's voice sounded like it was coming from the left.

Harri and Dan walked through the trees towards Richard.

"One last time? Harri said.

"Over here," Richard said. His voice was much closer.

"I see him," Dan said.

He led Harri out of the trees and into a small clearing. Richard stood in the middle of it, his back to several small buildings surrounding a larger two-story building. It was impressive for such a remote location. The structures looked like log cabins. Very rustic. The boys must have been so excited to come here. Especially since many of them were from broken homes and foster care.

The completeness of the camp surprised Harri. It must have really been done well. "How many boys were here when you were?" Harri asked.

"There were eight of us. And Lauren. We all stayed in that building." He pointed to the smaller building to the left. "All the videos were made in the mess hall. That's what they called it," Richard added.

"What was that building for?" Dan asked pointing to the smaller building on the right.

"Those were for the overnights," Richard explained. "John and Paul organized those. And George was the one that got us," Richard's voice came out hollow.

"I'm so sorry we have to stay here," Harri said. She couldn't imagine how difficult being here must be for him.

"Let's go there," he said, pointing to the building he'd said they'd bunked in.

Harri and Dan followed Richard as he pulled open

the door. The stench of mildew escaped into the fresh, clean air.

She gagged and pressed her fist to her mouth.

"It smells awful," Dan said.

"It's only for a couple more hours," Harri said. "It must be after midnight by now."

Richard reappeared. "We can't stay in there. They left all the beds and things are growing in there."

"Let's do the mess hall then," Harri said.

Richard nodded and headed towards the hall.

Suddenly, a soaking wet man stepped out of the shadows of the hall. Dan gasped, and Harri instinctively reached for her gun, which wasn't there. In a flash, the man put a gun to Richard's head.

"Hello, old friend."

39

DAY 6 - NIGHT

Dirt and water whipped into Jake's face as the police helicopter attempted to land on the small strip of beach. It was the third try as the first two had been unsuccessful. Jake was dripping wet from all the lake water whipped up by the intense wind created by the helicopter blades. His teeth chattered as the helicopter inched closer and closer to the ground.

POP!

POP!

Jake's heart thumped as he heard the shots. What was happening on that island? Was Harri trying to take down whoever held Dan or was it the other way around?

The helicopter door opened, and the pilot waved them inside. Jake picked his way around the rocks and climbed aboard. Gavin was already yelling and gesturing toward the island.

Jake buckled up in the small back seat. Gavin stayed up front with the pilot. The helicopter took off and Jake's stomach flopped around like a dying fish on a dry dock.

He hated flying in helicopters. His motion sickness activated immediately.

He gripped the seat with both hands and held on. The lake below them was like glass, sharp, and beautiful. The loud THUMP THUMP THUMP of the helicopter blades drowned out any other sounds during their short journey.

The helicopter descended towards the rocky shore and Jake fought not to puke. He unbuckled his seatbelt, ready to disembark the moment the helicopter touched ground.

Jake was thrown forward as the pilot hit the beach with too much velocity.

"Sorry about that," the pilot called back.

Jake waved him off, already on his feet, and opening the door. He jumped down onto the rocky beach. Out of the corner of his eye, he saw Gavin do the same. With his Glock poised and ready, Jake stalked into the woods, listening for any sounds that could tell him where the fight was happening. As he walked further away from the helicopter, he heard screaming. He picked up his pace.

"Slow down, Jake. We don't know where the shooter is," Gavin called to him.

Jake knew that, but he still plunged in, all his thoughts on Harri.

40

DAY 6 - NIGHT

Harri urged Dan to move, but Robert Payton must have seen her small gesture.

"Don't even think of running, bitch. He'll be dead on the spot and I'll pick you both off before you can reach my boat."

She'd seen him before. It was the man from the mall who'd picked out clothes for a boy already dead.

"I've seen you before. At the mall," she said.

Keeping the gun pointed at Richard's head, Robert Payton turned to her.

"You didn't react to the gifts I left in your room."

"So, you were following me."

Harri wanted to pull his focus, to keep it on her. As long as he was looking at her and talking, she knew Richard and Dan had a fighting chance.

"I was leaving the mall when I saw you," he said. "I didn't realize you'd be buying new clothes so soon. I saw an opportunity and I took it."

"You chose those clothes, the red sweater, and khakis

for Alan Prentiss," Harri said. "You did that, so I'd know it was you. That was quite a risk." Harri acknowledged.

If she kept him talking, then she might get an opportunity to disarm him. She let go of Dan's hand.

"I wanted you to see me," Robert said.

"Why?" Harri asked as she inched closer.

Richard struggled and Robert viciously yanked him back. Dan stood frozen where he was, his eyes on Robert and Richard.

"Because you finally made the connection, Harriet." Robert snickered. "You finally figured it out about the camp and what happened here. You came every year to look for your sister and yet you had no idea. You never had a clue the answer was right under your nose."

"Why did you kill Chris Becker?" Harri asked.

"I didn't kill Chris Becker. He wasn't one of mine," Bobby said.

Harri wasn't sure if she should believe him or not. She tried another gambit.

"You could have come to me," Harri said, keeping her eyes on his gun. "You didn't need to kill those boys."

As Robert spoke, the gun swayed around Richard's head. She could use her body to push him away from Richard if she could get close enough. The pain in her shoulder screamed, but she pushed it back, all her focus on Richard.

"I wasn't a bad boy, but I was punished."

"What did that have to do with me?" Dan suddenly screamed.

"I was going to make you clean and nice," Robert said.

His voice had changed. The pitch increased slightly. Harri waved her hand behind her back trying to get Dan to stop talking. She wouldn't be able to control the situation if Dan got Robert angry.

"What does that mean?" Harri asked calmly.

"He mouthed off to me," Robert told Harri as if he was reporting Dan's misbehavior. "He mouthed off to me, his Professor. He has no respect for authority. Look what he's put his parents through? Look how he treats his own body."

Robert spoke directly to Dan. "I was going to teach you a lesson so the same thing wouldn't happen to you," Robert said.

"Why did you kill Atticus Menlo?" Harri asked, hoping to steer the focus away from Dan.

Harri met Richard's eyes. Her eyes moved to Robert then back to Richard. He nodded his head. She hoped he understood she'd try to take her chance whenever she found an opening.

"I couldn't make him clean," Robert explained.

"Clean like you became clean. After what happened here?" Harri asked.

Robert's face screwed up in anger.

"I will never be clean," Robert said vehemently. "This place. You don't understand. They did things to us and we will never be the same."

Robert jerked Richard back again. "Those boys had a chance, and they didn't take it. They didn't understand that when you get a chance, you have to take it. You won't get another chance. They were mouthy and didn't deserve..." He stopped.

"Deserve what?" Dan spewed.

The anger in his voice was palpable. He was cracking. If Dan put himself in harm's way, then Harri was stuck. She couldn't take the chance of throwing herself at Robert if Dan could get hurt.

Harri put her hand up to stop Dan's movement forward.

"Do you know why they killed my sister?" Harri asked. "Richard told me some of it," she added, keeping her voice as calm as possible. "But maybe he doesn't know the whole story?"

Robert hesitated. He looked at Richard and then back at Harri. This is what he claimed he wanted.

"Something happened to their operation," Robert said. "I heard them yelling to each other. They needed to clear out but couldn't decide what to do with us. Your sister was a big problem for them. No one would believe us. We were delinquents, throwaways. But your sister…"

Everyone was quiet for a moment. Harri heard something far off in the distance. In the quiet of the woods, she thought she heard what sounded like a helicopter. She listened again, but the sound was gone.

"They had to kill her," Richard continued. "Lauren never tried to escape before. No matter what they did to her. All they ever had to do was threaten one of us and she always did whatever they said. But she convinced us to run that night."

"All except for Tanner. He was small and too scared," Richard added.

"So, she picked him up and carried him while we ran," Robert said.

"We didn't get far," Richard continued.

"They hunted us like animals," Robert said, his anger growing.

Harri imagined how terrified her sister must have been that night. How desperately she must have wanted to get away, but she couldn't leave a little boy behind. Harri put her hand on her chest feeling her heart break apart.

"When was this? The fall of 1994?" Harri asked.

It was almost time. She could tell both men had pulled back into the past and she hoped Robert had loosened his grip on Richard and forgotten he was holding a gun.

"No. The summer of '95." Richard said.

Their theory had been correct. The photo was from the summer of '95. They'd had her sister for almost a year. A year where she must have endured so much horror and pain.

"How did you ever get away? Who were these men?"

"The shots were ringing out everywhere," Richard explained. "Bobby and I swerved off the path and sprinted through the woods. We reached the beach and jumped right in. The water was so cold, but we kept going. We left them all behind," Richard whispered, his tone horrified, his guilt seeping through every word.

"We just wanted to get away, to get off the island like Chris had."

"You both were only boys," Harri said.

"Why did you take me then?" Dan screamed. "After all that happened, why would you do this to other people?"

He wasn't going to be still any longer.

"I never touched you, did I?" Robert said, pointing the gun at Dan.

"Put the gun down, Bobby," Harri said trying to diffuse the situation.

"I didn't touch any of those boys," Robert said through gritted teeth. "I never hurt them. I'm not like Chris. I made them clean."

"Give me the gun, Bobby," Harri said as she extended her arm.

She wanted all his attention on her. He pointed the gun at her.

"I know what you're trying to do," Robert sneered.

Richard took that moment to strike. He threw himself at the gun.

"Get down," Harri yelled and threw herself on Dan. Her collarbone exploded with pain as her body hit Dan's. They both fell to the ground.

Harri watched as the two men struggled for the gun. Richard was losing ground. Harri left Dan on the ground and rushed to help Richard.

She was halfway to them when the gun went off. Richard's face crumpled in pain. He'd been hit. Robert fumbled for the gun, but Richard grabbed it from him.

The gun went off again, this time hitting Robert. Both men fell. Harri crawled over to Robert. The blank look on his face showed he was dead.

"Oh, my god." Dan whimpered behind her. "Oh, my god. Is he really dead?"

Harri glanced back at Dan. He crumpled to the ground, sobbing. She turned to Richard and took his hand. Blood spurted from his mouth. The bullet must have hit the lungs.

"Hang in there, Richard," Harri pleaded. She squeezed his hand and watched his eyes flutter. His lips moved and Harri kneeled closer, straining to hear his words over Dan's sobs.

"I should have stopped him. I knew it could have been him when the first boy went missing. I hoped it wasn't."

"This wasn't on you," Harri said. "You got away. You saved us. You're a good boy."

Richard's breathing was shallow. He was slipping away.

"Tell me who did this to you?" she begged. "Who killed my sister?"

"John, Mark, George," he whispered as his eyes closed for the last time.

"No!" Harri cried. "Please, no. Richard!" Harri shook him, but he was gone.

"Harri! Harri!" Jake's voice sounded behind her.

Harri shook her pounding head in disbelief. She must be worse off than she thought. Then strong arms enveloped her, and she cried out in pain.

She heard Jake's voice in her ear. "I found you."

Harri cried out in pain. Her shattered collarbone sent shockwaves of pain through her body. "Broken. I'm broken."

Jake cradled her gently as Gavin checked Dan. She was safe. Jake had found her. With the last thoughts, she let go and drifted into the comfort of painless darkness.

41

DAY 10 – OCTOBER 6, 2018

Harri Harper turned her face to the sun as the motorboat bumped along the lake to the small island where the NecroFind team had been working all morning.

Her collarbone was set, and her arm was in a sling. Medication dulled her pain, but she was careful not to overdo the dosage because of her concussion.

The night of the rescue still remained a partial blur to her. She remembered Jake's arms around her, but little else. She woke up in the hospital the next morning with contraptions holding her arm just so and a bandage around her head.

After a battery of tests on both her head and body, Harri had been discharged with warnings about avoiding hitting her head and keeping her arm in a sling until her collarbone healed. Jake stayed by her bedside the entire time she'd been there.

Tim, Molly, and Dan visited her in the hospital as she recuperated. Tim tearfully hugged and thanked her. Dan looked like the ghost of himself in daylight, but he didn't have the hunger in his eyes that she'd seen on his friends at the 7-Eleven. Harri hoped he'd stay clean. He deserved a second chance.

Detective Gavin French and Detective Robinson had been some of her last visitors. They'd found evidence at Robert Payton's house conclusively linking him to Dan Ledeyen's abduction and the deaths of Atticus Menlo and Alan Prentiss. The case was closed as Robert Payton was dead. Yet, they were still collecting evidence and wanted to interview her.

Gavin made sure he was the one to tell her about NecroFind. He'd been authorized to invite them to the island to search for the graves of her sister and the six boys that Richard Miller claimed died at the same time.

That's where the motorboat was taking her. Jake sat by her side, holding her hand in his.

"Are you ready for this?" he asked her.

"Yes and no," Harri admitted.

"I feel the same way," Jake said. "Are you going to be okay going back there?"

"What do you mean?"

"PTSD, that sort of thing."

He said it awkwardly and Harri appreciated his checking in on her like that.

"I'm fine," Harri assured him. "I'm anxious to see what they've found."

This boat trip was the culmination of twenty-five years of searching, all her training as a cop, and her belief she would someday bring her sister home.

"How many graves have they found?" Harri asked as the boat slowed.

"Nine," Jake said.

Harri couldn't take her eyes off the tree line. She

could see white tents through the trees and crime scene techs milling about.

The boat skimmed onto the beach and Jake took Harri's hand. "Let me help you out," he said.

He maneuvered himself to the beach and reached back for her. Harri allowed him to lift her out of the boat and set her on the rocky shore. She steadied herself against him and took his hand again as they headed toward the NecroFind workstation.

Dr. Susan came out of the trees.

"I've been watching out for you," she said and hugged Harri.

"You've found some remains I've heard," Harri said.

"Indeed, we have. If you'll follow me," she said a small smile playing on her face.

Harri took the lead and Jake held her hips to steady her as they picked their way through rocks and fallen branches to the burial site.

Harri could see the main cabins of the camp to the left some two hundred feet away. Dr. Susan turned to the right and led her to a small clearing filled with the NecroFind team and the crime scene technicians.

A white canopy had been constructed over the nine partially uncovered graves.

"Is she here?" Harri whispered.

Tears filled her eyes as she looked at the bones of the children in front of her.

"We've found the remains of what appears to be an older teenager," Dr. Susan confirmed. "A female."

Harri turned to Jake. "We did it. We found her."

"We can bring her home now," Jake said as he caught her up in an embrace.

They held onto each other as the teams of technicians

worked in front of them. Harri nestled her head on his chest, her heartbeat against Jake's.

She knew this was still an unsolved case. Now, she had to find justice for her sister and these boys who nobody had ever come looking for.

But for now, she'd take the win. She'd found Dan and brought him home and she'd found her sister. She smiled at the thought of Lauren walking free through the woods. She imagined her surrounded by the seven boys and the smallest one in her arms. Lauren turned, smiled and waved, and led the boys into the trees.

"What is it?" Jake murmured.

"Thank you," she said.

"For what?" He laughed.

"For everything," she said. "For coming back to me. For being you."

"I'm so glad I did, Harri," he replied. "I'm so glad I did."

I hope you enjoyed reading The Hidden Grave! Detective Harri Harper's new case is back in Los Angeles in The Broken Trail. Click here for Book 3!

ALSO BY DOMINIKA BEST

Harriet Harper Thriller Series

The Creek Killer

The Hidden Grave

The Broken Trail

The Night Blinder

Ghosts of Los Angeles Series

The Haunting of Sunshine House

The Haunting of Eva Murphy

The Haunting of Alexas Hotel

Detective Harriet Harper returns in
The Broken Trail

ABOUT DOMINIKA BEST

Dominika Best is the author of the Harriet Harper Thriller Series and the Los Angeles Ghosts series.

For more information:
www.dominikabest.com
hello@dominikabest.com

Made in United States
Troutdale, OR
09/06/2023